the

Heart Reader

of Franklin High

the Heart Reader

of Franklin High

TERRI BLACKSTOCK

W PUBLISHING GROUP™

www.wpublishinggroup.com

A Division of Thomas Nelson, Inc.
www.ThomasNelson.com

Published by W Publishing Group, a Division of Thomas Nelson, Inc., P.O. Box 141000, Nashville, Tennessee 37214 in association with the literary agency of Alive Communications, Inc., 7680 Goddard Street, Suite 200, Colorado Springs, CO 80920.

Scripture quotations are from The Holy Bible, New International Version (NIV). Copyright © 1973, 1978, 1984 by International Bible Society. Used by permission of Zondervan Publishing House. All rights reserved.

This novella is a work of fiction. Names, characters, places, and incidents are either the product of the author's imagination or are used fictitiously. Any resemblance to actual events, locales, organizations, or persons, living or dead, is entirely coincidental and beyond the intent of either the author or the publisher.

ISBN 0-8499-4369-8

Printed in the United States of America

02 03 04 05 PHX 6 5 4 3 2 1

At this, the man's ears were opened, his tongue was loosened
and he began to speak plainly.
MARK 7:35

one

Jake Sheffield knew what it was to fall over the edge. Weeks ago, he had fallen out of his canoe at least a dozen times on the youth trip down the Ocoee River, first by accident, then several more times just to get a good laugh. Some faux genius who enjoyed seeing him out of control—probably a freshman trying to fit in to the youth group—had photographed one of his falls for posterity and left the snapshot in his seat tonight. He'd heard a flurry of snickers from the back of the room—the freshman section—as soon as he had sat down. He had studied the picture himself, muffling his own laughter, then passed it to Andy, who snorted like a sow and passed it to Logan.

Gary, the youth pastor, sat on a stool at the front of the room, his guitar on his lap. He was dead serious and getting emotional as he talked about some passage in Luke where there were a bunch of lost things. He'd made a big deal earlier of calling the roll and noticing that Tim James was missing and taking off to look for him with the whole youth group trailing behind. No one had been fooled. Gary had never called the roll before, so they knew this was some kind of sermon illustration, and they just went with it. Anything to keep from sitting on those hard folding chairs.

Now that they had found Tim, who'd been hiding behind the Coke machine and had jumped out like a psycho and scared some of the girls, Gary had them back in the youth room and was trying to make his point.

"Anybody know why Jesus told this parable of the lost son?"

The sophomores who took up the first row tried to look dumb so he wouldn't call on them. Jake's sister, Heather, seemed to be deeply interested in a hangnail on her index finger, but Jake knew she was probably running the question through her mind and trying to come up with the right answer. She couldn't stand to be wrong or, worse, ignorant. The juniors on Jake's row were still nudging one another about the picture. The seniors, sitting along the side, unwilling to commit themselves by mixing into the group, looked at them as if they already knew the answers but were giving others a turn.

Some brave, unenlightened freshman in the back spoke up. "To show that home is where the heart is?"

Jake glanced back and saw who had made that feeble attempt at intelligence. He shot her a look that said that answer was inane. She seemed embarrassed, but he knew she liked it. Having a junior shoot her an insulting look was close to being included.

Gary was a master at pretending any answer made sense. "Home is where the heart is. Okay, that may have been one of the points. Anybody else?"

Jake couldn't help laughing. Gary was too nice to tell anyone they were wrong. He thought of a great Christmas present for the youth minister this year—a buzzer that he could push, with some obnoxious honking noise that went off when someone gave a stupid answer. He wrote it down on the handout Gary had given them with Luke 15 on it. He thrust it at Andy. Again, he snorted.

"It's about it never being too late to come back," Mason MacMillon said in his harsh voice.

"Yes!" Gary said, as if Mason had just answered the winning question on Jeopardy. "Guys, what Jesus wanted us to know is that every single one of us is important. That if there's even one lost, he'll leave the others to go looking for the lost one. That's why he told us about the lost sheep. The shepherd left the flock to find the one lost sheep. The woman turned the whole house upside down looking for the lost coin. How does it feel to know that God isn't content with the flock? That he cares enough to come looking for you?"

Andy passed the note about the buzzer down to Amanda, and she smirked and showed it to Matt, next to her. He leaned forward and flashed Jake a grin and a thumbs-up.

"So if we're vessels of Christ, if we're supposed to be working for and with him, what should we be doing?" Gary went on.

"Looking for coins?" Ben Harper, a senior, asked. Everyone laughed.

Gary didn't mind. He was like a kid himself, always horsing around with them and not afraid to get dirty. One of the times Jake had gone over the canoe, Gary had pretended that he was trying to save him and had gone in after him. He had practically drowned Jake in his attempt, and that had gotten even a bigger laugh.

But tonight he was on a roll. "Specifically, we should be looking for lost people. Christ came to seek and to save that which was lost, guys. And as his children, we should be doing the same." He lowered his voice the way he always did when he wanted them to lean in, listen hard. "To do that, guys, we have to start hearing like God hears. We have to hear their needs. We have to hear their souls crying out. We have to believe that we have the cure, the map home, the answer to all their questions."

The snapshot had made its way to the back row, and Jake heard some chuckles back there. Gary just kept talking. "People, listen. This is important. I'm starting a class on evangelism. Soul winning. I want those of you who feel you need to learn how to share your faith to come to this class tomorrow afternoon. It'll only be an hour, right at first. We'll learn some Scriptures that will help you witness to your friends, and we'll talk about ways we can reach people at school and all around us. It's at four-thirty right here tomorrow. I need all of you I can get. After a couple of weeks, we'll start going out to practice sharing our faith . . . on real people." He paused for a moment, as if waiting to see if anyone would jump out of their seat and beg him to sign them up. When no one did, he slapped his knees. "Now, let me see that picture. It must be good."

Jake felt a little embarrassed. He always thought Gary couldn't see what they were passing around. He hoped it hadn't hurt his feelings that they'd been doing something besides listening. After all, it was as if they were living in two separate universes sometimes—Gary at the front of the room in his spiritual mode and them in the seats, dealing with reality going on around them. If anybody understood that, Gary did.

Gary found the picture and burst out laughing. He held it up. "Everybody see this?"

The group rolled in laughter, and several of the kids made wise-cracks about Jake finally getting his. "Thank goodness I saved him!" Gary shouted. "Jake, did you see a doctor about that vertigo? He just couldn't stay in that boat." Jake stood up and took a bow as the group chided him, then he pretended to lose his balance again and tip over.

When Gary could be heard again above the commotion, he raised his hand to get their attention. "Let's close with a prayer, guys!"

He practically had to yell the prayer over the snickers about Jake, and the minute he said, "Amen," Brandon, at the back of the room, pressed the play button on the stereo and started the Supertones cassette.

As the youth got up and began gravitating into their cliques, the transition from spiritual quiet to reality's deafening roar was quick and easy.

two

That night, reality faded again in the recesses of Jake's sleep, and he had a dream. He was in it, yet he was only a spectator, standing back and watching. He saw his grandmother milling around her house, looking for something under her cookie jars and behind her toaster, picking up rugs and kicking aside trash cans. She was always losing her keys, he thought, so his eyes swept over the tabletops and hooks on the wall. He saw them hanging right where they were supposed to be, but she walked right past them and kept searching.

And then she wasn't his grandmother but some strange woman he didn't know, and she was getting frustrated and upset, searching, searching . . .

She cried out in joy as she saw what she had been seeking and fell down to grab it. It was a quarter. A stinking, lousy quarter, and Jake wanted to tell her that she'd wasted a lot of time and precious energy going to all that trouble for something that wouldn't even buy a burger.

Quickly, he was jolted from the old woman's grandmother-house to a field full of sheep. He saw a shepherd there, with a long sheet over his head, like something out of *The Ten Commandments,* only the shepherd's face was Gary's face. He had lost a sheep, and Jake figured the sheep looked like Tim James and that it was hiding behind the Coke machine. But Gary didn't look as cheerful as he'd looked when they'd gone on their fake wild-goose chase earlier at church. Tonight, he looked distraught, and he left the flock to go and look for the lost sheep. He was breathing hard and fighting thorns and branches and tripping over logs and bushes in his search. He was sweating, and Jake followed him, wanting to pull off the sheet so he wouldn't be so hot and tell him to look behind the Coke machine.

The shepherd turned around, frantically searching, but it wasn't Gary anymore. It was some strange, sweaty guy who looked like he would bust a gut if he didn't find that sheep. And there wasn't a Coke machine in sight.

Jake stood back and watched, perplexed, as the shepherd kept looking, getting farther and farther from the sheep, getting more and more frustrated and breathing harder and sweating more. Behind him, Jake could hear the flock, and he wondered if the shepherd was just going to leave them all there.

Finally, he heard a shout, and the shepherd began to sing and rejoice. Then he emerged from the brush with a baby sheep in his arms, and on his face Jake saw tears of joy as he ran back to the flock with the lost sheep.

Jake knew he was in a dream, and he felt like he was under water, waiting as the water lifted him up, up, up to the place where he could draw in a breath of air. But just before he reached the top, he heard a voice, mighty and strong. *"Ephphatha!"*

The voice brought him completely awake, and he sat upright in bed, gulping air. He was sweating, as the shepherd had, and his hands were shaking. *It was a dream,* he thought. *Just a dream.*

He lay back down, but he was too wired after the dream to go back to sleep. He looked at his clock, saw that it was 5:00 A.M. He still had an hour and a half before he had to get up, but he wasn't too interested in falling back into that dream. Something about that voice . . .

He whispered the word again, just as the voice had said it. It wasn't a word he knew or had ever seen or heard before. What did it mean? Had it come out of one of the dark folds in his brain, like some kind of psychic hiccup? He reached for a pen and wrote out the word. He didn't spell it the way it sounded, but somehow, he felt it was right. *Ephphatha.* What did it mean?

He got up and went into the kitchen. His mother was still in bed, but his sister, Heather, was up, about to head out to swim team practice. The early hour they had to practice was exactly what had kept Jake from going out for the team. But Heather was one of those driven types. She hardly ever slept. She was up when he dropped into bed at night and was usually up when he woke in the morning.

"What are you doing up so early?" she asked.

"Couldn't sleep." He went to the refrigerator and perused the contents. He wondered if the milk was sour. He looked over his shoulder and saw that she was drinking some, so he figured it must be all right.

"Guilty conscience?" she asked. "What did you and your reprobate friends do last night?"

That was just like her. She was a little thing, standing in her team bathing suit with a big shirt over it that swallowed her up. Her long blond hair was pulled back in a ponytail, and those big blue eyes made her look sweet and innocent. But looks deceived.

"You tell me who has a guilty conscience," he said. "You're the one who never sleeps." He poured a glass. "I had this dream . . ."

"Really? What was it?"

"Something about a sheep. And a quarter." He looked down at the tiles on the counter. "And it felt like somebody . . . God, maybe . . . was talking to me."

She began to hum the tune to "The Twilight Zone." "It was probably those anchovies on the pizza last night," she said. "Fish give bad dreams, don't they?"

"It wasn't bad, really," he said. "Just weird."

"I told Gary that nobody likes anchovies, but for some reason, he keeps ordering them. Guess he wants to keep reminding us about being fishers of men."

Jake padded barefoot to the pantry and looked in for some cereal. "Yeah, that's Gary," he said. "There's a lesson in everything. Even the little guys on our pizza."

"I could stand to catch a few fish."

He looked back at her. "Then go fishing."

"Hmmm?" She was finishing her own cereal, and her mouth was full.

"Go fishing."

"No, I'm going to swim team practice." She took her bowl to the sink and dropped it in with a clash. A horn sounded outside. "That's Jeanie. Gotta go."

He didn't say good-bye. He was too busy trying to figure out why she'd mentioned fishing in the first place.

Since Jake was already up, he decided to head to school early and work on the term paper that had been looming over him like a dark funnel cloud. School didn't start until eight, but the librarian got there at seven for those industrious students who wanted to get a jump on things . . . or the procrastinators who had waited until the last minute to get started.

He stopped inside the library door and looked around at the people who got here so early. There was Byrd the Nerd, a.k.a. Steven Byrd, who had been clinging to the number one rank in his class since they'd started keeping track. Jake couldn't relate. He was ranked ninety-five or something, out of a class of two hundred. At another table was Trina Bradshaw, cheerleader and sophomore class beauty. She was the glamorous type and wore a black sweater with a mink collar which she admitted she had salvaged from her grandmother's attic. He had been interested in her since the beginning of the school year, but she was out of his league. To keep from looking like a lovesick puppy, he headed to the table where Lee Grange, the school's star quarterback, sat. Though Jake hadn't made the football team, he got along okay with the jocks because he played baseball with them in the summer. He dropped his books onto the table and scraped the chair back, defying the silence in the room.

Mrs. Whittle, the librarian, looked up at him over her glasses. He held his hands up in an apologetic gesture, and she went back to her work, no doubt reading about the nesting habits of ants or some such thing. Exciting lady.

"I have to win."

Jake opened his notebook and started flipping pages. "Yep. Important game tonight, all right."

Grange looked up at him, an irritated expression on his face, as if he didn't want to talk about it. He went back to the book he was reading, so Jake did too.

"Losing is not an option. He didn't raise a loser."

Jake looked up again. "Who didn't? Your dad?"

Grange looked puzzled . . . at least, as puzzled as he ever allowed himself to look. He was big on intimidation, even with his friends, and didn't like to look stupid. "Who're you talking to, Sheffield?"

Jake sat back in his chair. "You. You said he didn't raise a loser. I'm just trying to get things into context, okay?"

Grange's eyes narrowed as he stared at Jake. "I'm trying to read. You mind?"

"Fine," Jake said, getting annoyed. "If you don't want to talk, then don't talk. I don't have a problem with that."

Grange pinned him with that intimidating stare, then finally, he went back to his book.

"I can't be a loser."

Jake was getting aggravated. He slammed his book shut and leaned forward on the table. "Grange, I thought you didn't want to talk!"

Grange's teeth came together, and his lips snarled back as if he was staring down a middle linebacker on the two-yard line. "Why don't you just shove your nose back in your book, Sheffield?"

Jake's mouth fell open. "What is your problem?"

Grange stacked his books and got up. He crammed his things into his backpack and, cursing under his breath, stormed out. Jake held his hands up innocently and glanced around him, looking for anyone who could tell him what he'd done wrong. The girl sitting at the table next to them looked up but didn't seem that interested.

He sighed hard and went back to reading.

"It isn't worth it. I could just make a clean exit." The girl's voice reached him like a whisper.

He looked over at her. What was her name? Beth? Bess? Or maybe it was Emily. Or Elizabeth. She was a plain-looking girl who was easy to miss. "What do you mean, a clean exit?" he asked.

The question seemed to startle her. "Huh?"

"What you said."

"I didn't say anything."

He grunted. "Why do people keep saying stuff and then claiming they didn't?" He couldn't study in such a hostile environment. He got his books, thrust himself up, and marched out through the library doors. He almost ran head-on into a Goth, dressed in a black tee shirt and black jeans. He had dyed his hair black, but his roots were blond.

Thick black eyeliner encircled his eyes, making his face look pale. It was an odd look, but Jake supposed it got the message across, whatever that message was.

"They're gonna know my name," the Goth said. "I won't be anonymous anymore."

Jake froze. He knew he'd heard the words, but he was looking right at him, and the kid's lips weren't moving. Jake stood there, stricken, blocking his way. The kid pushed past him, bumping him aside with an insolence that dared him to protest.

Slowly, Jake walked out into the school commons. He saw Andy, his best friend, in a huddle near the library door.

"Hey, Jake."

Jake walked slowly toward him, still puzzling over what had just happened. "Andy, do you know that Goth that just went into the library?"

Andy looked through the glass door. "Yeah, that's Zeke. He's a sophomore. A real loser."

"Did you hear him say something just now?"

Andy shrugged. "I heard a lot of people say a lot of things."

"But something about being anonymous?"

Andy shook his head. "Hey, did you hear about Grange losing it at football practice last night? Coach said he might pull him out of the starting lineup tonight."

Jake started to tell him about his confusing exchange with the quarterback, when he heard Andy's voice again.

"I don't feel very holy."

Again, the words were coming, but his mouth was moving to a whole different conversation about football and first-stringers. "Did you hear me, man?"

Jake thought he was going to be sick. "Uh, I'll be back in a minute."

He headed for the bathroom, but as he passed Greta Holiday, he heard her say, "I need to lose ten more pounds. Just ten more pounds and everything will be perfect."

He shot her a surprised look. She was already ninety pounds, nothing but bones and joints. But again, she wasn't talking to him . . . or to anybody else.

He ran into someone and backed up. "Excuse me."

"I can't erase it. None of it. It's all written out, and it'll never change."

Jake looked up at the guy whose name he didn't know. He struggled to find something to say, something like, "Could you tell me where everybody's getting their ventriloquism lessons?" But before he could get the words out, the guy was gone.

Jake was really sick now. But instead of heading for the bathroom, he went to the pay phone. He fished in his pocket for the money and inserted it. His hands were shaking as he dialed his home number.

As it rang, Trina Bradshaw came sashaying up to use the phone. "Are you gonna be long?"

"No," he said. He was beginning to sweat like he had after his dream. He hated for her to see him like this.

"I have to keep busy, have to keep moving, have to go, go, go . . ."

He turned back around and looked at Trina just as his mother answered the phone. She was just standing there, combing her fingers through her big brown hair.

He clutched his head and turned his back to Trina so she couldn't hear. "Mom? I'm sick. Yeah, I feel like I'm gonna throw up. I need to come home. No, you don't have to check me out. School hasn't started yet. I just . . . wanted to let you know before you went to work . . . No, I think I can drive. I'm okay. Yeah."

"Gotta keep going, gotta talk, gotta go, gotta move . . ."

He looked back at Trina, astonished that she would have those frantic thoughts running inside her like a tape that kept repeating itself. Then it dawned on him—was that it? Was he hearing her thoughts? Was he listening in on her private emotions?

He couldn't handle it, not even with Trina. He could use inside information on her, but not while he was sweating and shaking like Barney Fife. Life was becoming a foreign movie with badly dubbed voice-overs. It was too bizarre to be real. He surrendered the phone and fled from the building as fast as he could.

three

Jake's mother had gone to work by the time he got back home, and he unlocked the door and went tentatively in. He had to admit he'd been spooked by the voices he'd heard. He checked out the kitchen, then went into the living room and scoped it out, making sure no one was hiding behind the curtains or under the tables, waiting to jump out and . . . what? Talk to him without moving their lips?

This was just too weird. He finished searching their house for anything out of the ordinary but found no life except for his pet iguana, Simon, the gerbil that Heather kept in her room, and some type of bacterial culture growing out of a dirty glass on his computer table. Nothing that could talk.

It was quiet, almost too quiet, so he sat down at the kitchen table and tried to think. The day had started out crazy. He'd had that dream and thought God was talking to him. And then he'd heard Grange and the girl next to him, and that Zeke dude, and Andy . . . and Trina, saying things they hadn't really said.

The phone rang, and he jumped a foot out of his chair. It was on the third ring before he'd caught his breath enough to answer it. "Hello?"

"Jake, are you all right?"

It was his mother. He thought of telling her that he was losing it, that they needed to send a psychiatric ambulance before he flipped out entirely, but she had enough problems. "Yeah, I'm okay," he lied.

"Do you want me to come home?"

"No. I'll be fine." He was starting to perspire again, and he wiped his forehead.

"I was thinking I probably needed to call the doctor. What were your symptoms again?"

Headache, trembling, hearing voices. He realized that this could get out of hand. His mother never took an illness lightly. He could picture himself sitting in the doctor's office this afternoon and the nurse listing his symptoms in his file. Yeah, they'd all take that real seriously.

He sighed and rubbed his eyes, trying to figure out just how to word this so it wouldn't freak his mother out. "Uh, Mom, I don't really know how to say this, and I don't really want to talk about it right now. But I don't think I'm really sick. I mean, not like I said at first."

"You lied?" his mother asked. "What . . . do you have a test today that you didn't want to take?"

He closed his eyes. "No, Mom, nothing like that. It's just that I've been a little upset about something. I was really feeling sick when I called, and I'm not feeling a whole lot better now, but I don't think it's physical."

She was silent for a moment and then asked, "Is it a girl, Jake?"

"I wish." He dropped his face into his hand. "No, Mom, it's not a girl, it's just . . . look, I'd really rather talk about this with somebody else."

"Jake, you know you can tell me anything."

"I know, Mom, but there are just some things that a guy needs to talk about with . . ."

"With a man?" she asked.

He knew that dagger would plunge too deeply, and he didn't want her to be hurt. She was very sensitive about their dad not being in the home. "No, that's not what I meant, Mom. It's not a guy thing. Just . . . maybe a spiritual thing." Yeah, that sounded good. "Maybe a spiritual advisor is what I need."

"Spiritual advisor?" She sounded alarmed.

"Yeah, like Gary."

That seemed to relieve her. "Thank goodness. For a minute there I thought you were talking about some New Age guru or something."

"No. Just . . . maybe Gary could help me."

She hesitated again, and he could tell she was trying to decide whether to be hurt or not. "Well, okay, if you think it'll help. Go ahead and see him. I'm sure he's in the office today. I think he sleeps there or something. He's there almost all the time, day or night. I don't know when he sees his family." She seemed to think that over. "Tell him not to work so hard, why don't you?"

"Okay. And Mom? Don't worry about me, okay? I'm fine."

"Okay, but Jake, I want you to promise me that if you start feeling better you'll go back to school. You can't afford to miss a day for no reason."

"Trust me, Mom, there is a reason," he said.

He got back into his car and drove the few minutes to the church he attended. There were a few cars in the parking lot, and he wondered if he would have to explain to anyone why he was there. He hoped not.

He saw Gary's car and breathed a sigh of relief. Quickly, he got out and went in. Matilda, the secretary, who'd been working there for eight hundred years, looked up at him over her reading glasses. "May I help you?" she asked.

He knew she didn't know his name, probably didn't even know that he'd gone to this church since birth. She was busy at the moment, writing down an order from the Tupperware catalog she flipped through.

"Uh, yeah. I need to see Gary, please."

"Sure . . . Gary . . ." She searched the telephone for Gary's extension as if no one had ever called him before. She seemed surprised and pleased when she found it. "Gary, there's a young man here to see you." She looked up. "What's your name again?"

"Jake. Jake Sheffield," he said.

"Jake Sheffield," she repeated into the phone. And then he heard the words.

"What about me? Why am I always last?"

He frowned and stared at her, stricken. She was still talking into the phone to Gary, saying nothing about being last. He started to feel sick again and backed away from her desk. He bumped into someone hurrying in the door and swung around.

"Jake, how you doing?" It was the pastor, Brother Harold.

"I'm okay," Jake said, starting to perspire again. "I just needed to talk to Gary for a minute."

The pastor looked down at Matilda, his raised eyebrows asking her if she'd taken care of Jake. She adjusted her glasses and nodded. "Gary is coming."

"Good to see you, Jake," the pastor said, patting him on his back.

"I need to understand more, need to dig deeper."

The words assaulted Jake, like a wave of icy water, and he caught his breath. Again, the pastor's lips weren't moving to the words Jake was hearing. "I'm looking forward to the dance Gary has planned for next month. Thought the wife and I would come and see if we could learn a few steps."

Jake just gaped at him, unable to follow the rambling. It was the other voice that had snagged him.

"Jake? Jake, are you sure you're okay?"

"Yeah, sure. I'm just a little . . ." He couldn't find the word and looked over at Matilda. He still felt as if he was going to throw up.

Thankfully, Gary burst into the room just in time. "Jake, what you doing here, man? Why aren't you at school?"

Jake just stared at Gary for a minute. "Um . . . I need to talk to you."

Gary's smile collapsed, and Jake saw the instant concern on his face. "Sure, man, just come on in here where we can talk."

The pastor backed off, and Matilda went back to her catalog as Gary ushered Jake back to his office. The youth minister's domain was small and filled with paraphernalia and posters, study guides and CDs. His desk was covered with paperwork, and Jake frowned, wondering how in the world he had time to plan anything with so much stuff to take care of.

Gary cleaned a stack off of a chair and gave the seat to Jake. "Sorry about the mess," he said. "I was just putting packets together for the youth conference we've got coming up."

"No problem," Jake said, dropping into the chair.

Gary took the swivel chair behind his desk and turned it around to face Jake. They were almost knee to knee in the little room. "So what's going on, man? You look like you just got dissed by Trina Bradshaw or something."

Jake knew he shouldn't have confided his crush on Trina to Gary. He'd figured that it was safe since she didn't go to church here, but Gary referred to it on a weekly basis. It was his way of bonding, Jake supposed. "Man, I don't know what's happening." Tears stung Jake's eyes, but he told himself he wasn't going to cry. He hadn't shed a tear in years, couldn't even remember the last time. It was probably around the time his parents told him they were splitting up, but even then, he didn't remember openly weeping like he wanted to do now.

His mouth was shaking at the corners, so he covered it and tried to wipe the expression away. It was clear that Gary was getting very concerned. He leaned his elbows on his knees and gazed at Jake. "Man, something's wrong. You've gotta tell me. What is it?"

"I'm losing it, Gary," Jake said. "Something really weird has been happening to me today, and I don't know what to make of it. I'm hearing these voices everywhere I go. They're just coming at me out of nowhere."

Gary's face was still for a moment, but then his brows furrowed deeper, and he sat up straighter. "What do you mean, voices?"

"People, like, talking to me, only they're not talking to *me*. I don't know who they're talking to . . . I can just hear them."

Gary was trying hard to follow him, but the effort was futile. "You're gonna have to slow down, Jake. I can see that you're upset, but—"

"They're thoughts, emotions. I don't know. I just hear these voices. Even out there with Matilda and Brother Harold—I heard their voices."

"Man, I heard their voices too. I've always heard their voices. What's the problem?"

"Not their regular voices! Gary, listen to me, I'm trying to tell you. It's not their words. It's not what they're saying. It's something else."

Gary's face changed, and he sat back hard in his chair, regarding Jake as the wheels in his head seemed to turn. "Jake, I know you don't usually get high . . . that's not your style . . . but today, did you do anything different on the way to school?"

"No, man, I'm not on drugs!" Jake jumped up from his chair, unable to believe his youth minister would think such a thing about him.

"How long have you been this way?" Gary asked, still trying to dig to the bottom of the problem.

"I woke up this way. Well, sort of. I mean, this hasn't been a normal day from the beginning."

"I'm listening," Gary said.

"It was the dream," Jake said, turning his back to Gary and walking around the small room as he spoke. "Before I even woke up, I had this insane dream. It didn't even make any sense. There was my grandmother, looking for a coin or something. She found some stupid quarter, but she tore her whole house up looking for it. And then the guy with the thing over his head."

"What thing?"

"A sheet. You know, like a shepherd. He had this whole flock of sheep, and he took off looking for the lost one . . ."

Gary's eyes suddenly changed, and Jake saw a hint of amusement there. "Oh, now I see."

"You do?" Jake asked, turning around. "What do you see, Gary?"

"Did you fall asleep reading Luke last night, by any chance?"

Jake's hopes deflated. "No, man, why?"

"Then maybe it was what I said in Bible study last night. Remember? I talked about the lost coin, the lost sheep, the lost son. Remember Tim James got lost, and we went looking for him?"

"Yeah, yeah, I remembered all that," Jake said. "I made that connection right away. But there was something else. See . . ." He combed his fingers through his hair. "See, I had that dream, and it was kind of frustrating, and then I woke up, and I heard this voice, just out of nowhere, and I could have sworn it was God talking to me."

"God talking to you?"

"Yes," he said. "Gary, I know how this sounds, and believe me, there's nobody else I would have said this to outright. Anybody else would have had me committed, but you . . . I just thought maybe you'd understand. Maybe you'd know what was happening."

"So this voice you heard," Gary asked, still looking disturbed, "what did it say?"

"I wrote it down." He pulled it out of his jeans pocket and handed it to Gary. "*Ephphatha*. Ever heard that before?"

Gary shook his head. "Are you sure it's spelled right?"

"Pretty sure, but I don't know how I know that. I was thinking that . . . if it was God talking, maybe it was Hebrew or Greek . . . I mean, I know he speaks English and everything, but his language of choice is probably one of the biblical languages, right?"

Even as he spoke, Gary got up and began perusing his bookshelves. "What are you looking for?"

"The concordance," Gary said. "I have one for Hebrew and Greek. Maybe it's there." He found the book, pulled it out, and started flipping the pages. "I hope it's spelled right. Course, if it was God, I guess he would have given you the correct spelling."

Jake threw his hands up. "Look, I know you think I'm nuts. You *should* think I'm nuts. If you didn't, I would think *you* were nuts. And I'm not sure it was God. It just seemed like it was. But I haven't told you the rest, Gary." He propped his foot on the chair and leaned in to make Gary listen. "See, I went to school early because I got up early, and I figured I'd go to the library and work on my paper, and I get there and sit down next to Lee Grange, the quarterback . . ."

"Yeah, I know Grange."

"And, anyway, Grange is sitting there, studying, minding his own business, and all of a sudden I start hearing this voice saying he's a loser and how he can't lose, how his dad—or whoever—didn't raise a loser. I almost got in a fight with him, because when I answered him, he claimed he hadn't said anything to me. He gets up and leaves mad, and I'm sitting there, and this girl next to me starts rambling, and I answer her, and *she* gets all offended."

"What did she say?"

"Man, I don't even remember. I was getting freaked out by that time, so I got up and bumped into some Goth walking in, and he's talking about being anonymous and everything . . ."

"Anonymous?"

"Yeah, I don't know. Only he didn't say it. It wasn't something he *said*."

"But you heard the words."

"I heard a voice. It was his voice, but . . . Then I went out into the commons, and everybody was standing around, and I could hear voices all around me."

"So you were hearing their thoughts?" Gary asked.

"No, not their thoughts. At least, I don't think it was. I mean like, Trina Bradshaw was standing next to me, but I couldn't hear what she thought of me. It wasn't like I could read her thoughts."

"So what did you hear?"

"Stupid stuff, like she was doing this 'I-gotta-go-gotta-move-gotta-go' stuff. This frantic chanting. And there was Andy. He was standing there saying that he didn't feel very holy, only can you imagine Andy saying a thing like that? And that was the thing. He *didn't* say it. It was like . . . their feelings. Gary, you've got to help me."

Gary looked down at the concordance in his hands, and his jaw started working. Jake knew he had put him in a bad spot. It probably wasn't that often that one of his students came in and started talking crazy like this, dropping the ball into Gary's lap as the adult in the picture. Gary was probably wondering whether to just go ahead and call the men in white coats.

"Jake, have you talked to your mother about this?"

"Well, not really. She knew I came to talk to you. But I told her it was personal. I don't want her to get all upset and scared over this."

Gary nodded. "Well, Jake, I think the thing to do is to get you an appointment with a counselor. I think your mother's gonna have to be brought in on it."

"But she's not strong enough right now. I mean, she was in this relationship, and I think she was hoping for marriage, and then they broke up, and she's been depressed and moping around the house. I hate to bother her with it."

"Jake, you're her son. It's not a bother."

"But how would you feel if little Hannah started hearing voices?"

"She's only three. She hears all kinds of voices. She has an imaginary friend we set a place for at night."

"It's not the same thing, and you know it."

Gary sighed. "Yeah, I know. You're right." Gary regarded Jake carefully again. "Man, are you sure you haven't been playing around with dope? I mean, you could say it if you were. You wouldn't be the only kid in the youth group who's ever messed up."

"No, man! I don't do that stuff. This is not drugs causing this. It's something to do with that word. Go ahead, look it up."

Gary started flipping through the concordance again. "Maybe somebody slipped something in your drink and you didn't know it."

"I'm telling you, I'm not high."

"I'm not called to this. I have no impact."

Jake turned around and saw with dread that it was happening again. Gary's mouth wasn't moving. Instead, he was flipping through that book, his eyes still full of concern, yet his voice was speaking.

"I have no impact. No one listens. There's no fruit."

"Man, you just did it!" Jake said, pointing at Gary as if he'd caught him picking his nose.

Gary jumped. "What do you mean? Did what?"

"You did it! I heard your voice. You were talking, but you weren't moving your mouth."

"No way," Gary said.

Jake plopped down in the chair. "You said that you weren't called, that you didn't have an impact, that there wasn't any fruit . . ." His face fell as the words sank in. "You're not about to quit, are you, man?"

The concern fell off of Gary's face, replaced by a look of shock. He simply stared at Jake for a long moment. "Man, I haven't told anybody that," he whispered.

"You just told me," Jake said.

"I didn't say that. How did you know?"

"I told you, I can hear those things. That's what I'm talking about."

"But I must have said something to plant that in your mind. I must have given some indication."

"No way," Jake said. "No way in a million years would I think you'd give up being a youth pastor. Man, I thought you were a permanent fixture in this church. I can't believe you'd think about leaving us."

Gary held up a hand to quiet him down. "I haven't made the decision to leave, okay? And I'd appreciate it if you'd keep it between you and me, especially since I didn't tell you in the first place." His face was reddening as he flipped through the book some more. "Course, I don't guess it's such a stretch that the idea would be planted in your mind, since I don't have an impact and nobody does listen to me. Maybe everybody's figured it out."

"Gary, don't you get it? You didn't plant it in my mind. Haven't you heard a word I've said?"

Gary stopped flipping and looked up at him again, and finally, his face drained of its tension. "Guess I need to listen differently, if you really heard that." He drew in a deep breath and looked back down at the book. "It's here. The word is here. *Ephphatha.* It's Greek, and it appears in Mark 7:34." He grabbed his Bible and opened it to that book, and Jake came to stand behind him. They both skimmed the passage.

"Oh, boy," Gary said. "This is incredible."

"What?" Jake asked.

"This is the place in the Bible where somebody brought Jesus a deaf, mute man, and Jesus spat on his fingers and stuck them in the man's ears, and he said, *'Ephphatha!* Be opened!' And the man began to hear and speak."

Jake shook his head. "Man, I don't think I have ever read that."

Gary looked up. "You haven't read the Gospels?"

"Pieces. Matthew and John, I think. And some other books. My point is not that I'm a heathen, but that I've never heard that before. It couldn't be unconsciously planted in my mind or anything."

"And I didn't mention it at youth group last night."

"So God said it to me this morning, and it meant, 'Be opened.' But what? What does he want to open?"

"Your ears, apparently," Gary said. "I mean, if what you're saying is true . . ."

"It's true, man."

"Then God spoke to you, and all of a sudden, you started hearing voices."

"But why would God make *me* hear this stuff?"

Gary sat back, trying to figure it all out. Finally, his face got that "aha!" look. "Remember yesterday, in my message to the youth, I talked about what would happen if we could hear with God's ears? If we could hear their spiritual needs, know what God knows?"

"Yeah," Jake said, though he didn't remember a word of it. He'd been too busy passing the picture and note around.

"Maybe this is a gift, Jake!"

"A gift? Man, now I know you're off base. This is no gift."

"But what if it is? Jake, what if God has given you something that lets you hear people's deepest needs? What if God has done exactly what I suggested yesterday? If he's given you ears to hear what he hears?"

"He wouldn't pick me. Your theory is blown right there. He would pick somebody like you, somebody who would know what to do with it. The whole concept was your idea, anyway."

"You know what to do. You're a Christian," Gary said. "You know what to tell people."

"No way, man. Not me."

"Why not you?" he asked. "He picked Moses, and Moses didn't know why. He picked David, a little shepherd boy, out in the field. He picked Peter, a fisherman, and Paul, who went around killing Christians. Why couldn't he pick Jake Sheffield, student?"

"Because I'm not like Moses or David or Simon Peter. I read my Bible when it's convenient, usually so I can argue a point. I don't know enough. I believe in Jesus, but it's not like I'm ready to go take on the world. I'm like one of those baby Christians that still needs milk."

Gary grinned. "I can't believe you'd admit that. Not the guy who spent two hours debating with me over how God would fulfill Armageddon."

"Man, I just knew enough to argue that. It doesn't mean I'm some spiritual genius that God would want to use."

"God likes weakness in his instruments. That's one of the ways he works. He picks the weak so he can show his own strength."

Jake got up and turned his back to Gary. He didn't want to hear this. "Man, you're way off. Way, way off."

"Think about it," Gary said. "Just think back over the things you've heard people say today. Could they have been their spiritual needs?"

He thought back over Grange sitting at the table talking about being a loser and the girl next to him and the Goth and Andy in the hall and Trina. He thought of Matilda and the pastor and Gary . . .

He wanted to cry again. He turned slowly back around. "Yeah, I think they would definitely qualify as spiritual needs."

Gary's face lit up. "Then, don't you see? What I wouldn't *give* to have a gift like this. Jake, you're so blessed!"

"Blessed? Gary, this is a curse. What am I supposed to do with it?"

"Maybe you're supposed to meet the needs you hear. Maybe you're supposed to talk to them about Jesus, tell them what you know."

"Man, I can't believe God would pick a seventeen-year-old punk who's never told anybody about Jesus, except for my pet iguana, who, I might add, did not listen very carefully."

"You gotta tell more than your iguana," Gary said on a chuckle. "You gotta tell the ones God lets you hear."

"Man, they'll laugh me out of school. I can't do that!"

"But witnessing is what we're all supposed to be doing," Gary said. "Don't you understand that? Church isn't something that happens a couple of times a week, in some building after we've sung a few songs and are feeling all sweet and charitable. That's what I've been trying to tell you guys. This is supposed to work in every area of our life!"

Those tears that Jake had been fighting pushed through. "Man, I don't even know what to say. I don't know what to do! Am I just gonna keep hearing people's voices coming out of nowhere and think I won't wind up in a straitjacket?"

Jake dropped his face into his hands, and as the tears came harder, he felt himself shaking, felt his face heating up. He wanted to get out of there, but he didn't know where to go.

Gary touched his shoulder. "I'll help you, Jake," he said. "You and I will go out today, and you can tell me what you hear, and I'll kind of take it from there, and you and I together, we'll see exactly what the Lord has planned."

Jake still couldn't look up at him.

"Look at the bright side, man. A few minutes ago, I thought you were crazy. I don't think that anymore."

Jake started to laugh and looked up at him. "You were ready to get somebody in here with a tranquilizer gun, weren't you?"

Gary laughed. "No kidding, man. But this is an awesome thing."

"You wouldn't think it if it were you."

"Well, it's not me. It's you. You have a choice. You can let it eat away at your brain and convince you you're not sane. Or you can go out there and make yourself a willing vessel. I can help you."

"Where would we go?"

"We could go to the mall. Maybe the arcade, after school. Just see what you hear."

"But I don't want to hear. I want to stay in a quiet room where there aren't any voices."

"But think of each one of those voices as a lost soul. A voice crying out to you for help. You're the only one who knows how to rescue them. It's like they have a disease and you have the only cure."

"Man, don't put this guilt trip on me."

"God never gives you a gift he doesn't equip you to use, Jake. You can handle this." He stood up and took Jake's hand, urging him to his feet. Jake wiped the tears off his face, but he was afraid more would come. He hated to walk out into the office and let Matilda see him blubbering like an idiot. He was glad she couldn't remember his name to tell his mother.

"Man, God is sure going to regret pulling me into this equation."

Gary only smiled. "When are you gonna learn, Jake? God doesn't make mistakes."

four

Jake's headache had just about disappeared by the time he met Gary after school was out. He had gone home in the meantime, had spent the day lying on his bed in the quiet, trying to decide what in the world had come over him and what he was supposed to do about it. As the quiet hours passed, he began to convince himself that what he'd heard had all been in his imagination. None of it was real.

Still, doubt lingered like the remnants of his headache. As school hours ended, he knew that Gary would be looking to meet him at the arcade, and if he didn't show, Gary would think he was a coward.

The parking lot outside the mall was already beginning to get crowded. He found a parking place and sluffed inside, not looking forward to what was ahead of him. He braced himself as he stepped through a crowd, praying that he wouldn't hear the voices. But then they came.

"I could vanish and nobody would notice. I'm practically invisible already."

He turned around and saw a kid standing outside of a crowd, smiling as if he belonged, but Jake knew he didn't. He kept walking, looking for Gary. He pushed through the food court where a group of guys his age stood in line, waiting to order.

"I'm sick; I'm dying, a second at a time . . ."

He swung away from the group, not even willing to meet the eyes of the person whose need he'd heard. As he got several yards away, he threw a look back over his shoulder, then bumped into a girl in a brown Hamburger Haven uniform.

"Excuse me," he said. "I wasn't watching where I was going."

"No problem," she said.

"I can't have this baby. I've gotta do something, get rid of it, before anybody finds out."

He froze and looked at her. He could see that she'd been crying—the rims of her eyes were red. He started to say something about what he'd heard, but realized how stupid anything that came out of his mouth right then would sound.

"Uh, you okay?" he asked.

She shrugged. "Yeah. You didn't hurt me. No big deal."

He watched as she headed to one of the competing fast-food stands, got a Coke, then went to a table and sat down alone. She was waiting for someone, he thought. Was she waiting to tell them she was pregnant, that she had plans for that baby?

He ripped his eyes away from her and scanned the crowd for Gary again.

"Jake!"

He heard his name across the room and shifted his gaze until he saw Gary waving at him. "How ya doin', man?" Gary asked, cutting between tables. "You feeling any better?"

Jake hadn't realized he was shaking until he took Gary's hand. "No, it's still here. I'm still hearing it."

"Then, let's go to the arcade."

He grabbed Gary's arm. "No, that's too crowded."

"Well, we want it to be crowded. That's where you'll hear things."

"I'm hearing things here," he said. His voice was wobbling, and he knew those stupid tears would push into his eyes any minute, and he was going to look just as wimpy as he'd looked this morning heading out of the church.

"So what'd you hear, man?"

"I don't know," he said. "I don't want to talk about it."

"You look like you could use a drink." Gary ushered him to a table much too close to the girl he'd heard. "Let me go get you a drink and we'll just sit here and chill for a minute before we decide what to do."

Jake watched the girl as Gary approached a counter and ordered their drinks. She looked depressed, miserable. But he was quickly distracted by the other voices around him.

"There's no such thing as love. I'll never have it. I have to create it myself."

"If only someone would listen. But no one will listen, no one will listen, no one will listen . . ."

He was looking back over his shoulder, trying to figure out who felt they couldn't be listened to and which one wanted to be loved, when Gary came back to the table.

"Here you go, man."

"Thanks."

Gary sat back down and leaned in conspiratorially. "So tell me what you're hearing."

He sighed. "Somebody behind me thinks they'll never be loved, that they'll have to create it themselves."

"Who?" Gary asked.

"I don't know. Not sure. Then there's this other one—the guy directly behind me, I think—who wants to be listened to." Gary started to get up, but Jake stopped him. "No, man. There's another one. There's a girl over there. See the one in the brown uniform at the table next to us?"

Gary looked over his shoulder. "Yeah, what about her?"

"Well, I bumped into her . . . and I think she's pregnant."

"Really?" Gary looked back at her again. She couldn't be more than sixteen years old. "What makes you think that?"

"Because I heard her say something about a baby and how she had to get rid of it. She's sitting there now like she's waiting for somebody. Maybe she's gonna tell him."

"Did you tell her not to get an abortion? Did you talk to her about Christ having a plan for her life?"

Jake breathed a laugh. "No, of course I didn't. I just bumped into her. I happened to overhear something I wasn't supposed to hear. I'm not gonna turn around and start preaching her a sermon. She's got enough problems."

Gary just stared into Jake's face. "Jake, tell me something. Why do you think God let you hear her?"

"I don't know," Jake said. "To make me crazy?"

"Why would he do that?"

"I don't know. Maybe my future's in a padded cell. Maybe this is how he plans to get me there."

"You know better than that," Gary said. "Jake, God let you hear her voice because he wanted you to help her."

"Me help her? How could I help her? I don't know anything about her."

"Well, if she's pregnant, you know a lot. Just go over there and strike up a conversation. You've got inside information. You can get her talking."

Jake shook his head. "No way. What would I say? Excuse me, but I heard you thinking about being pregnant . . . ?"

"No, you don't have to be that blunt. Just go up to her and ask her if she's waiting for somebody."

"She'll think it's a pickup line. I don't even use pickup lines on people I want to pick up."

He saw a group of guys from his school coming in, crossing the food court. "Oh, great. There're some of the seniors from school. Now what am I gonna do?"

Gary looked back over his shoulder. "What do you mean, what are you going to do?"

"I mean, I'm gonna look like a fool. I can't do this."

"They're not even coming over here," Gary said. "They don't know what you're doing."

"But I don't want to start going up to people and saying strange things to them. They'll start laughing at me. It'll get around."

Gary's hopeful expression faded. "None of what I've been saying has gotten through. None of it." His lips didn't move again, and Jake knew he'd just heard one of Gary's thoughts.

"It has gotten through, Gary. Everything you've said has gotten through. You just don't understand."

It took Gary a moment to realize that Jake was responding to his deepest thought. "You heard me think that, didn't you?"

Jake nodded.

"Jake, don't you see what a gift this is? I would give anything for this. I don't know why you won't listen, why you won't use it. God gave this to you. I feel such a responsibility to help you use it right."

"It's not your responsibility," Jake said. "Just because I'm not some kind of evangelist doesn't mean I don't listen to you. I've heard everything you've ever said to me."

"How can you hear me when you're busy passing around pictures, whispering, and writing notes?" Gary asked.

Jake sat back hard in his chair. "Man, you've never said anything about that before. I'm not bothering anybody when I pass stuff around."

"It's distracting," Gary said. "They don't hear a word I say when you're doing that. And while we're on the subject, have you ever stood up in front of a group of people who couldn't care less what you had to say, people who looked down at their laps because they're writing notes to each other or reading something or passing pictures around, whispering? Have you ever stood up there and experienced that, Jake?"

Jake's brows came together in sudden shame, and he looked down at the table.

"Because I do every single time I get up in front of you guys. So don't tell me you've heard everything I've ever said. If you've heard even ten percent of what I've said, I'd be thrilled. But I don't think you have."

"Man, I shouldn't have come to you. I thought you, of all people, would understand what I'm going through, that you could help me."

"I'm trying to help you," Gary said. "I'm trying to show you what to do with this gift God has put in your hands."

"I don't want a gift," Jake said. "I never asked for one."

"Sometimes you get them without asking," Gary said. "That's one of the beautiful things about God."

"Then how come I feel like I'm being punished?"

"What do you think you're being punished for?"

Jake shrugged. "I don't know. Maybe what you just said. Because I don't pay attention in youth group. Because I'm distracting other people. Maybe he's trying to show me . . ."

Gary grabbed Jake's hand and stopped his rambling. "Jake, I think the only thing God wants to do is show you what he hears. He wants you to respond the way he would respond. He wants you to listen. Can't you listen?"

"I can't help listening," Jake said with tears rimming his eyes.

"Then, you have a choice," Gary said. "You can be miserable, thinking this is some kind of a curse and a punishment, or you can do something with it and help somebody. But to do that, you might have to go out on a limb. You might have to embarrass yourself a little. Do you remember when Moses sent Caleb and Joshua and the other spies into the Promised Land to scope it out?"

"Sort of," Jake said.

"Well, they went in and saw how big the people were and how mighty their army looked, and what did the spies say when they came back?"

Jake didn't have a clue. "I don't know."

"Ten of them said that the people were like giants and that the Israelites looked like grasshoppers against them. Caleb and Joshua, on the other hand, said that they could take them, simply because God was on their side. But the people chose to believe they were grasshoppers instead of giants, and they refused to go in. There's a lesson there for us, Jake. We're giants who think we're grasshoppers. But you are not a grasshopper, Jake."

"I feel like one. Like a worm, even. Like a worm crushed under somebody's shoe."

"But that's not what you are. You're a giant, and you have God fighting your battles."

Jake looked over at the girl. He could tell she was starting to cry. Apparently, she was being stood up. Jake felt sorry for her. But he wasn't about to hop over there and be the one to do anything about it.

"All right," Gary said, plopping his palms down on the table. "If you won't do something, I will."

And before Jake could say anything else, Gary got up and headed toward the girl.

Jake reached for his youth pastor to stop him. *"Gary!"* Gary didn't turn back. Jake wanted to scream that this was so unfair, that he'd never asked for any of this, but Gary wasn't interested. He was too busy introducing himself to the girl.

"Hi, my name's Gary Sullivan," Jake heard him saying, "and I'm the youth pastor at Mount Calvary Church. Are you waiting for someone?"

The girl wiped her tears as she looked up at him. "Yes."

"Well, would you mind if I kept you company for a minute while you waited? I'd just like to talk to you for a second."

She hesitated. "I guess it's okay."

"What's your name?" he asked.

"Beth Ann."

"Beth Ann, I was just sitting over there talking to a friend, and I glanced over and saw that you were crying. Anything you want to talk about?"

"Not to a stranger," she said.

He leaned forward on the table. "Beth Ann, there's something I don't know how to say to you, but I'm just gonna ask you to trust me here, okay?"

She waited with dull eyes.

"I can't tell you how or why, but I can say that the Lord has revealed to me that you're in kind of a mess right now."

Her eyes widened, and she sat up straight in her chair. "How do you know that?"

"Beth Ann, do you think you're pregnant?"

Jake turned to get a look at her pale face as she brought her hand to her mouth. "How did you know? I haven't told a soul. Not a single soul."

"Beth Ann, God knows. You can't keep secrets from him."

She started to cry harder, and Jake felt sorry for her. He wished Gary would just let up and leave her alone. It was a dirty trick, really. Hitting her with something like that without telling her how he really knew.

"Beth Ann, did you know that you're a child of the King?"

She was still crying, shaking her head. Jake listened more carefully.

"Really," Gary said. "A child of a King. You have an inheritance just waiting for you. A palace to live in. A family who loves you and has been looking for you. You have a Father who's so powerful that, with just a snap of his finger, he can do anything."

She dropped her head and covered her eyes as if she didn't want to see him as he spoke. "Yes, Beth Ann, you're a child of the King. Except you were separated from him at birth and raised by a family who wasn't royalty. They didn't know who you were. They didn't know you were special, that you had an inheritance, that you were chosen. And so they brought you up the best way they could. But they didn't have much, so you lived in squalor for most of your life. In poverty . . ."

Jake wondered what in the world Gary was talking about. He hadn't told him anything about the girl being some kind of princess. What was he trying to do?

The girl was as confused as Jake was. "I didn't grow up in poverty. And I'm not adopted. My parents are a normal, middle-class couple—"

"Just listen," he said, touching her hand. "Just hear me out."

She wiped her eyes now and looked up at Gary, trying to follow where he was going. Jake slid his chair back and turned, watching them both out of the corner of his eye. "You grew up in squalor," Gary continued. "There was nothing for you but struggles and pain. You felt like nobody. But then, one day, the King's men came to your house and knocked on your door and found you. And they said, 'Beth Ann, we've come to tell you that you're not living the life you were planned to lead. You have an inheritance. You're the child of the King.'"

Her face was softening as she listened.

"What would you do?" he asked.

She shook her head. "I'd tell them they were crazy, that they didn't know what they were talking about. That I'm just some kid who lives in a normal family and goes to school and makes mediocre grades and works a job nights to pay for the car she has that doesn't even run half the time. I'm not an heir to anything."

"But what if they could prove to you that you were and you refused to take it? Instead, you just couldn't believe it, so you kept living in squalor, struggling and striving."

She shook her head. "What has this got to do with my . . . situation?"

Jake wanted to lean closer, to say, "Yeah, what?" But he was out of the loop. He sat there waiting to see what Gary would say.

"I'm saying your life is not over. I'm saying that God is the King, and that he loves you, and that he wants to help you, and that it's not too late to join your true family and receive that inheritance."

"And what's that inheritance?" she asked.

"Eternal life. Life more abundantly on earth. Peace, even through crises like you're about to face." He leaned forward on the table. "Beth Ann, don't abort that baby. She or he is a child of the King too."

She wilted again. "But my parents will throw me out. My boyfriend . . . I think he suspects it, and that's why he hasn't shown up today. I think he knew what I was going to tell him. I'll be all alone . . . I won't know where to turn."

"That's not true," Gary said. "Our town has a Crisis Pregnancy Center. They can help you with your parents, and they can help you find a place to live if you need one. They can help take care of you until that baby comes, and they can help you decide whether to give it up for adoption or raise it yourself."

She dropped her face into her hands. "I can't be pregnant. If I am, my life for the next nine months is ruined."

"You're right, it'll be tough for about nine months," Gary said. "And if you decide to keep the baby, things'll never be the same. But aborting this child will stay on your conscience for the rest of your life. You'll never get over it. That's why the King doesn't want you to do it. He doesn't want you to be in that much pain."

"You think abortion is sin, but a lot of people don't."

"Depends on what you call sin," he said. "Sin, to me, is something that separates us from God. It's something that keeps us deceiving ourselves, so we'll never become who we're really supposed to be. God, the King, doesn't really want you to be separated from him, Beth Ann. He wants you to lean on him. He's not gonna condemn you because you lived in squalor, not knowing who you were. But now that you know, it's your choice. You can't be in the family and accept the inheritance, unless you *decide* to accept it."

"My baby will have nothing," she said. "Nothing. I can't give it anything if I have to drop out of school and work full time and lose the support of my parents . . ."

"You can give your baby everything," he said. "You can give your baby life, and you can tell this child about his or her inheritance." He reached into his pocket, pulled out his wallet, and found a business card he kept stuck there. "This is the address of the Crisis Pregnancy Center in town. You owe it to yourself, Beth Ann, to go there and see what your options are. See if they can help you."

"But my boyfriend will never speak to me again if I have this baby. We've talked about it before, what we would do if I ever got pregnant, and he said—"

"Beth Ann, just look into it. Give your baby a chance."

Sobbing, she got to her feet. "I have to go back to work. My break's over."

Quickly, he jotted his phone number on the back of the card and gave it to her. "Beth Ann, if you want to find out more about your true family, you let me know, okay? And if you want someone to go with you to the CPC, I'll be there to go with you anytime, night or day."

She stared down at the card. "Thanks. I appreciate it."

"Will you promise me that you'll go there and talk to them, just *talk* to them, before you do anything that can't be undone?"

She looked down at the card. "Yeah. I promise."

"Think about what they say, Beth Ann. Pray about it. Talk to the King. Your baby deserves that."

She hiccuped another sob, then headed back to the counter.

When Gary came back to Jake's table, Jake was awe-struck. "I can't believe you did that. That was so good. Did they teach you that stuff in seminary or something? Did they have classes on exactly what to say?"

"No," Gary said. "Of course they don't. I wouldn't have known what to say if you hadn't told me her need."

"But that thing about being a child of the King and part of the family . . . that was really cool."

"And really true."

"I know, but I would never have thought to say that."

"What would you have said?"

Jake shook his head. "I don't know. I've never thought about it much before."

"Well, why not?" Gary asked. "The Bible tells us to always be ready to give an account for the hope we have."

"But I've never really had to do that," he said. "I mean, most of my friends are from the youth group. They're already Christians. And the others, the ones I see at school and stuff, well . . . I think they know by my life, the way I act, that I'm a Christian. I'm nice to them."

"And you don't know any nice non-Christians?"

Jake thought about that for a moment. "Well, sure. There are lots of nice non-Christians."

"So why would they think you're a Christian just because you're nice?"

"Well, I don't cuss much. I don't do drugs. They know I'm active at church. Sometimes I wear Jesus tee shirts. They just know I'm a Christian. They can tell."

"But how many times have you ever said it out loud? I mean, there are lots of nice people in the world who don't know about Jesus. We can't be ashamed of our faith, Jake."

"I'm not ashamed," Jake said. "That's not it at all. It's just that I've never been confronted with it like this. I've never had to get up in some-body's face . . ."

"Is that what I was doing with Beth Ann? Getting up in her face?"

"Well, no, not really, but if I had done it, it would have seemed that way. Look, I'm not like you. Talking to people like that, it's not what I do. I mean, what if I had sat down with her and started talking to her, and she asked me some churchy question that I couldn't answer? Something about the Bible?"

"You could have answered it, Jake."

"No, I couldn't. I hate to break it to you, Gary, but I really don't know the Bible all that well." The admission instantly shamed him.

"Just tell her about Jesus, about her family, about her inheritance."

"Inheritance," Jake repeated. "It's not like I can pull out a check for a million bucks. I mean, let's face it, it's a concept that's hard to grasp, even for those of us who believe it."

Gary started to laugh. "Boy, he's got you snookered, doesn't he?"

"Who?" Jake asked.

"Satan."

"I am not snookered."

"Then stop letting him call the shots."

Jake sat back again. He couldn't believe how harsh Gary was being with him. He'd never expected that much of him before, but then, Jake had never had such potential before. At least not that he knew of.

One of the seniors from Jake's school sat down alone at a table beside him, with a tray piled high with onion rings and a thick cheese-burger.

"I'm on a roller coaster without a seat belt," Jake heard the guy say. He glanced over his shoulder. There was nothing to indicate that the guy was panicked as he had just described.

He turned back. Gary was watching him. "Did you just hear that guy say something?"

"Yeah, he sort of said he felt like he was on a roller coaster without a seat belt."

"Go tell him, Jake. Tell him he doesn't have to feel like he's in a train wreck. Tell him there's someone who can be in control."

Jake's headache was coming back. "Look, I know what you're saying, and I understand it. That God really is making me hear these things so I'll do something. But maybe it's just so I'll tell you so *you* can do something."

"No, Jake, that's not it. God gave this gift to you, not me."

"But what do I say? Do I just walk up and say, 'Hey, about those roller coasters without seat belts . . .'"

"Just tell him what Jesus did for you. Tell him who's controlling your life. I'm gonna go over here and talk to somebody. I see one of the kids I used to visit a lot last year."

Jake grabbed his sleeve. "Look, don't tell anybody, okay? Don't tell them anything about what's going on with me. I can't handle that."

"I won't. Just go talk to the roller-coaster guy, Jake," he said quietly. And before Jake knew it, Gary had left him alone. Jake sat there for a moment, looking around him. He felt as if everyone in the place knew what he was going through and was watching to see what he would do, but no one looked at him. No one at all. Not even Gary.

He whispered a silent prayer for God to help him, then got up and went to the table next to him. "Excuse me," he said. He cleared his throat, tried to make his voice come out more clearly. "Uh . . . I couldn't help overhearing . . ."

Roller-Coaster Guy shot him a look. "Overhearing what?"

Jake wanted to kick himself. Now what? He decided that he would get nowhere without honesty, so he pulled out the chair and sat down without asking and leaned in to the guy waiting for an answer. "I'm not even sure if you said it out loud."

The guy frowned.

"You said that you feel like you're on a roller coaster without a seat belt."

The guy's eyes narrowed.

Jake started to laugh. "You know, I realize how ridiculous this sounds. I mean, some guy you've never seen before—I do go to your school, by the way. I've seen you around. But to have me coming up to you and telling you that I just read your thoughts—"

"Read my thoughts?" the guy asked.

"Well, not really. I mean, it's not like I can hear what you're thinking or tell your future or anything. I mean, I'm not psychic."

The guy reached for the change he had laying on the table and slowly curled his fingers over it, as if he thought Jake had come to rob him. "Look, I know this is crazy," Jake said, talking way too fast. "But I just want to tell you that there was a time in my life when I felt like everything was out of control, like that roller coaster was gonna go over a big bump, and I would just start flying out into space. It seemed like my friends, my school, my life, everything, was out of control. Especially when I was with my friends. Man, I'd go out with them at night, and I'd get in their car, and we'd start heading out to wherever we were going, and I would feel less and less in control, and it was pretty scary."

The guy stared at him with his mouth hanging open, trying to follow the meandering thread of conversation.

"During that time, I got into some things that were really kind of bad. Part of it was peer pressure, but the other part, I think, was fear. I just wanted to feel better. I started to drink, and we were doing things that would get us into trouble. But I didn't care. I just needed that rush. Only it didn't give me that much of a rush. Afterwards, I just felt more out of control."

The guy seemed to be frozen, his eyes riveted on Jake. That encouraged Jake, so he kept on. "Then one day my sister—she's younger than I am, but she's sometimes a whole lot smarter—she came home and told me she'd started going to this church youth group and that she thought I needed to come. I thought she was out of her mind, but I went . . . and I started hearing about, you know, Jesus, and—"

"Hold it right there," the guy said. "I don't want to hear anymore."

"What do you mean?" Jake asked. "I'm just telling you what happened to me."

"I figured it was something like that when you sat down," he said. "People don't just come up to you out of nowhere and start talking for no reason. Look, just leave me alone. I'm not bothering you or anybody else. I just came here to eat."

"Sure." Jake got to his feet, a little confused. "I didn't mean to make you mad. I just wanted to tell you that you don't have to feel you're on a roller coaster with the seat belt unbuckled. I haven't felt like that since I became a Christian; I've had peace. Because of my sister, I came to know Jesus, and ever since, my life has been different, and I just wanted to tell you about it, because there aren't that many people I've told in my life . . . and as I was sitting there just now, I had this feeling that I needed to tell you."

Just then, the senior's friends surrounded the table with trays of their own, and they rattled down their food and took their seats. Jake wondered if that was why the guy hadn't responded. Had he seen his friends coming and didn't want to be embarrassed in front of them?

"Look, if you want to talk more, you can call me. Jake Sheffield, and it's the Sheffield in the phone book on Picard Avenue."

The boy took a big bite of his hamburger and chewed without looking at Jake. "If you don't leave right now, I'm gonna call security," he said with his mouth full.

The others looked up at him, as if trying to figure out what was going on.

Jake's heart sank. First try, and he had failed. "All right, I'll leave you alone. But look." He pulled a ballpoint pen out of his pocket and bent down to write his phone number on the hamburger wrapper. "If you ever do call and I'm not home, the best thing you could do for yourself is call my youth minister. His name's Gary, and he works at Mount Calvary Church over on Bishop Drive." He jotted Gary's name next to the church name, then backed up, realizing that the wrapper was going to get thrown into the garbage can just like the rest of what Jake had told him.

His head was beginning to hurt again, and he looked around at the senior guys, staring up at him as if he had invaded some secret club or something. He started to walk away.

He must have walked ten feet when the roller-coaster guy stopped him. "Hey, you!"

Jake stopped and turned around. "Yeah?"

"Thanks for telling me about Jesus!" The words were yelled at the top of his lungs, and Jake doubted that there was anyone in the food court who hadn't heard. The guys at the table erupted into laughter, and Jake looked around and saw others staring at him with disgusted grins on their faces.

He wanted to die.

He turned around and started walking toward Gary. He could see on his youth pastor's face that he had heard. Gary quickly excused himself from the person he was talking to and fell into step with Jake as he headed out of the food court.

Jake was quiet until they got around the corner. "I told you," Jake said. "I told you I couldn't do it. That it's not my gift, that I'd just mess somebody's life up if I tried."

"Who's life did you mess up?" Gary asked.

"That guy. If somebody who knew what they were doing had witnessed to him, maybe things would have turned out differently."

"Jake, you're the one God sent over there to talk to him."

"No, I'm the one *you* sent over there to talk to him. If you had gone, the guy would probably be signing up for seminary right about now."

"That's not true. Even Jesus didn't win everybody, Jake. All we have to do is be obedient. We do the best we can, and then we let God do the rest. You planted a seed just now. You have no idea who's gonna water it and who's gonna reap it. But trust me, the Holy Spirit has done a work today. You know, Ezekiel told us that we're accountable for telling people. If they hear us and they don't listen, then their blood is on their own hands. But if we know something they don't know and we don't tell them, their blood is on our hands."

"But I don't get it. Why wouldn't he listen if I told him exactly what his spiritual need was?"

Gary shook his head. "I'm not sure that people know what their spiritual needs are. Even when you confront them directly with something you know is in their heart, they're not always going to accept it."

"Then, what good is my hearing voices?" Jake asked. "I mean, I just made a fool out of myself and didn't do any good."

"You did good for the girl I talked to."

"The one who's pregnant? How? I didn't even talk to her!"

"No, but you told me what I needed to know so I could talk to her.

And I think she's gonna get help. I think what I did with her planted some seeds too."

"But this seed-planting business . . . You can't know how effective it is. I mean, what if we're just kidding ourselves about planting seeds, and what we're doing instead is just driving people away?"

"If we're people who have the Holy Spirit in our hearts and on our faces—if we're accessible and full of love and they can see Christ working in our lives—why would we drive anybody away?"

"I don't know," Jake said, "but we do it all the time."

Gary turned up one wing of the mall, and Jake followed automatically. "That's true. Well-intentioned Christians do seem to have a way of doing that. But maybe that has more to do with our being quiet than our being too vocal."

"What do you mean?"

"I mean, how many times have you missed opportunities to tell somebody about Christ, so they had to fill in the blanks about you and figure you out, and maybe they got the wrong impression."

"I've really never led anybody to Christ. Never even really wanted to, to be perfectly honest."

Gary grinned at his honesty. "I know how you feel. Really, I do. But we're supposed to multiply and bear fruit."

"But I'm not ready to multiply," Jake said. "I'm not ready to bear fruit."

"God's not gonna wait for you to be ready, Jake. Sometimes he just turns the ignition and puts it in drive. Sometimes he just drops you in a place where it's the only right thing to do. He's made it easier for you, Jake. Easier than for most people."

"This is not easy," Jake said. "Christianity will probably come to a crashing halt by the time God gets through with me."

"Not gonna happen," Gary said. "The gospel will go on without either of us to spread it. But for some strange reason, the Lord wants us to be a part of it."

five

Jake hadn't realized Gary was walking him to the arcade until they wound up there. The place was teeming with kids after school and blaring with music that competed with the sounds coming from the video games and pinball machines. Gary hesitated at the door before they went in.

"Okay, here's what we'll do," Gary said. "Since your confidence has kind of been shaken, I'll do the talking. All I need from you is for you to tell me what you hear. You can jump in when you feel more confident."

Jake appreciated the fact that Gary understood the pressure he was under. At least now he didn't have to worry about saying the wrong thing. He took a few steps in and stood for a moment, listening to the voices around him, the curses as people kicked and banged on the machines.

"Freedom's just another word for nothing left to lose."

He looked behind him and saw a kid who couldn't have been more than twelve years old. He had orange, spiked hair and was leaning against the wall, his arms crossed, watching the crowd. Jake nudged Gary.

"Did you hear something?" Gary whispered.

Jake nodded. "That boy against the wall said something about freedom being another word . . ."

"'For nothing left to lose'"? Gary grinned. "That's a line from an old Janis Joplin song. How does a kid that young know that?"

"Sixties parents," Jake said, listening. "Wait, there's more."

"Losers can lose even when they don't have anything to lose."

Jake turned back to Gary. "He thinks he's a loser. Says he has nothing left to lose, but then it was jumbled up . . . like, he thinks he can still lose something . . . even though he didn't have anything . . . because, you know, he's a loser."

"He's not a loser," Gary said, as if Jake had made the declaration instead of the kid himself. He stepped around Jake and walked up to the kid.

"Hi," he said, patting the kid on the back. "Why aren't you playing?"

The kid shrugged. "No money. I just like to watch."

Gary fished in his pocket and pulled out a dollar. "Here. On me."

The kid straightened. "Thanks, Mister."

"My name's Gary," he said. "Gary Sullivan. I'm the youth pastor at Mount Calvary Church over on Bishop Road. Haven't I seen you at our youth group?"

The kid shook his head. "I don't go to church."

"No wonder."

The kid shot him a look, as if his words surprised him. "What do you mean, 'no wonder'?"

"I mean, no wonder you think you're a loser. You haven't been told that you're a child of the King."

The kid started laughing. "Yeah, right. That's me. Prince Travis. And these are all my subjects."

Gary chuckled. "Man, you have no idea. You're so valuable that somebody was actually executed in your place."

The boy looked up at him, obviously wanting to hear more, but trying to appear nonchalant.

"You see it's like this," Gary said and leaned against the wall. The boy mirrored his stance and hung onto every word.

Jake felt as if he was intruding on a private moment, so he pushed through the crowd and headed for the concession stand. A black kid in a leather jacket with the word "Chaos" written on it—the name of the most violent gang in town—stood behind the counter. It surprised him that one of their members worked here. The kid wore four earrings in one ear and six in the other, and he had his nose pierced, as well.

"Whatcha want?" he asked.

"I'll just have a Coke," Jake said.

"The dark is gettin' darker, and there ain't light nowhere."

The words startled Jake, and he realized he was hearing the guy's thoughts. He didn't want to talk to him. Something about the way these guys in gangs strode around town, looking for trouble, had always seemed evil to him. Yet what he'd just heard told Jake that he had the same kind of longing that everyone else seemed to have.

"I'm turnin' into a shadow and blendin' in with the dark." The words sounded so dismal, so hopeless, that Jake looked back over his shoulder, hoping Gary was almost finished. He needed to come and talk to this guy, needed to share with him about where he could find the light. But Gary was still engaged in conversation with the Janis Joplin fan against the wall. Jake would have to do it himself.

But he took a deep breath and told the Lord that he couldn't, that it was too crowded in here, and that too many people would interrupt them at the concession stand, that he just didn't know what to say. When he looked at the guy again, he could see that no other customers were anywhere near the concession area. It was the perfect opportunity.

He cleared his throat and opened his mouth, hoping words that made sense would come out. "You ever lit a candle?" he asked.

The clerk turned back to him and handed him his Coke with the fizz running over the side. "Yeah, why?"

"You know how, when you light the match and light the candlewick and there's this little flame, it kind of smothers out all the darkness?"

The gangster looked at him, hanging tentatively on his words. "Your point?"

"My point," Jake said, "is that light can chase away the darkness. You don't have to let the darkness swallow you up."

The guy just stared at him for a moment, and Jake wondered what was going through his mind. Was he thinking about calling his Chaos buds over to smash his face into the floor? Was he trying to come up with just the right insult that would humiliate him appropriately in front of everyone? Or was he genuinely thinking over what Jake had just said?

Jake knew it was too late to turn back, so he just kept going. "You know, it doesn't matter how much darkness you bring into the light, it won't stay dark. And I know that sometimes you probably just feel that you're nothing but a shadow and that you're just going to blend into the darkness and cease to exist. That can't happen unless you let it. You have a choice. You can invite the darkness, or you can invite the light. And I've seen both, so I can tell you, the light is a whole lot better."

The guy's eyes seemed to soften, and he leaned on the counter. "Man, you don't know me. You don't know how dark it can be."

"I know how light it can be," Jake said. "Jesus Christ died to chase the darkness away. He said, 'I am the light of the world.' Maybe he was thinking of you when he said it."

The kid laughed out loud, and Jake began to brace himself. But then the gangster's humor faded and turned into a frown again. "I should have known you were leading up to something like that."

Jake leaned in. "Man, can I ask you something?"

"It's your dime," the guy said, as if that made any sense at all.

"Tell me why you would buy into the things you gangs do, why you'd want to dress in a way that scares old ladies, why you'd be interested in the occult and the Ouija boards and the things you guys like to do, and not even give one moment's consideration to the possibility that Jesus Christ died on the cross to set you free from sin."

"'Cause I don't need to be set free from sin, man. I ain't done nothin' wrong."

"Man, we've all done stuff wrong. I've done stuff wrong today. In the last hour. Probably in the last few minutes. You should have heard some of the things running through my mind about some guys who were at the food court."

"So why you think you're different from me?"

"I'm different because I know what the light is, and you don't."

"Dude, you don't know me."

"I know a lot about *me,* and I know where I was when I was thinking that the darkness was gonna swallow me up. It didn't, man. It doesn't have to. Light is a whole lot stronger than darkness."

The guy gave him that hard Chaos look again, and Jake realized that all it lacked was a switchblade to back it up. Then finally, those eyes softened again. "You know, sometimes, when I think about the stuff I do, I feel kinda like sucked in, you know, like there ain't no gettin' out."

"There's always a way out," Jake said.

"Yeah, but I be different from you," he said. "Dude like you, you can get religion, and then there's a place you can go, know what I'm sayin'? But they'd take one look at me and throw me out. They prob'ly got bouncers on the steps of the church, lookin' to throw dudes like me out."

Jake grinned. "Right. Angelic bouncers. Man, you're crazy. Everybody's welcome in my church."

The kid looked skeptical. "You sure about that, man? You tried bringin' a gangsta brother to your church?"

Jake knew he hadn't. His theory hadn't been tested, so he wasn't entirely sure. Then he decided he would make it true. "Yes," he said. "You can come to my church this Sunday if you want. In fact, that's my youth minister over there. Man, he'd jump up and down to see you there."

"Yeah, and I'll just bet everybody else would too."

"Try us," Jake said. "You're a guy who's not afraid to walk into the darkest places. Try walking into one that's well lit. Try coming with me this Sunday."

Jake looked him in the eye for a long moment, and as the gangster's features wilted, he saw the eyes of a young, confused boy, searching for something that had meaning. "I might take you up on that," he said. "Just to prove a point."

"Do," Jake said. "If I'm right, you owe it to yourself to find out. And if I'm wrong, well then, I need to know."

The gangster reached across the counter to shake Jake's hand. "You got a deal, man," he said.

"If you're coming, I need to know your name."

"L. J.," he said, pronouncing it *El*-jay.

"I'm Jake. I'll see you on the steps at 9:30."

"Nine-thirty? Dude, I don't get to bed till eight."

"Try going earlier. To prove that point and all."

The guy just laughed and began to wipe the counter.

It was all Jake could do to keep from screaming "Yes" and running to tell Gary.

six

By the time they left the arcade, Gary had led the Janis Joplin fan and two others to Christ, using the information Jake was able to give him. Jake still had not been successful except for the conversation he'd had with the gangster behind the counter. He didn't know what was wrong with him. Even with this alleged "gift," he couldn't get anywhere.

But Gary was on a high. "I want you to come to the hospital with me," Gary said as they got into his car. "I need to visit somebody."

"I'm not very good with sick people," Jake said. "Maybe I ought to just go on home."

"These aren't really sick people," Gary said. "To tell you the truth, it's a rehab."

"A rehab? You mean like for druggies and stuff?"

"For people trying to clean up their lives," Gary said.

"But who are you going to visit? There's nobody in our youth group in rehab."

Gary started the engine. "There's a guy named Lou MacLemore. His mom called me a few weeks ago and asked if I would start visiting him. He's been in a lot of trouble, and he's trying to break his slavery to drugs."

"Why did she want you to visit him?"

"Because she's a Christian and she hoped that I might be able to lead him to Christ."

"Have you been able to?"

"I'm not sure," he said. "See, he's been inoculated."

"Inoculated to what?"

"Christianity. He was raised in the church. He knows all about

Jesus. Claims he's a Christian, yet he's not taking hold of any of what is his in Christ. So I'm not sure where he really is."

"Why'd she call you if he already had a church?"

"Apparently he'd had some run-ins with his own youth minister, and she didn't think he'd be very effective in helping him."

This whole scenario was making Jake uncomfortable. "So, won't he be upset if I come along?"

"Actually I had been thinking about bringing some kids along to kind of introduce him to our youth group, so that when he got out, he might feel like he had some friends there and come along. I even asked him if that would be all right, and he said, 'Sure.' But I hadn't brought anybody yet."

"Why not?"

"Because I never could figure out which one of you to take. None of you seemed that interested in sharing your faith. I felt like I had a lot of work to do on you before I could take you to see him."

Jake was quiet. He hated the idea that he had let his youth pastor down when he needed such a simple thing. "Man, I'll be happy to go talk to him, but if you think I'm gonna be any help, you need to think again. I'm not good at this. The Hare Krishnas will be able to mop up everywhere I've been. I'll have people running to shave their heads."

Gary laughed. "You'll get better," he said. "Look what happened at the arcade with the guy at the concession stand. God doesn't give you a gift unless he plans for you to use it. And he's gonna teach you how. That's what today is about. All I want you to do today is come and make friends with this guy, but I also want you to tell me what you hear."

"Well, how do I do that if he's sitting right there? I can't talk about him right in front of him."

"Do what you have to do," Gary said. "I need to peek into this boy. I need to see what God sees. You can help me with that."

Jake groaned.

"And if you hear anything from any of the others, let me know."

"Other druggies?"

"Don't call them druggies, Jake. They're in bondage. They're getting help."

"But you know what I mean," Jake said. "I don't get along real well with people like that."

"People like what?" Gary asked. "These are kids like you, they just took a wrong turn somewhere, got with the wrong friends. Or they just made a mistake and then couldn't stop. Look at them the way God looks at them, Jake. Hear them the way God hears them. He's not giving you glimpses into their souls without a reason. He's trying to do something in you."

Gary drove quietly for a few miles, as Jake turned that thought over in his mind. If someone had told him yesterday that he would be visiting some stranger in rehab, hoping to tell him about Jesus, he would have told them they were crazy. Yet Gary must have done this kind of thing all the time.

He looked over at the youth pastor. "Is this what you do during the day? Visit people in hospitals? I mean, I'm not trying to insult you or anything, but I kind of thought you just sat around thinking up fun stuff for us to do. But you're actually out there going to hospitals and rehabs? Visiting people?"

Gary grinned. "My sole purpose in life, Jake, is that when I go to heaven I'll take as many people with me as I can. And don't look now, but that's your purpose in life too."

Jake rolled his eyes. "Don't know about that."

"Well, I've been praying that God would show you today."

Jake watched him as he drove. "Gary, I still can't believe you were thinking about leaving. I mean, you seem to be so passionate about your job, like it's a calling. It's something you're supposed to be doing."

"I'll keep doing it," Gary said, "whether I'm a youth minister or not. I don't have to be on the church staff to tell people about Jesus."

"No, but you love what you do. You have fun doing it."

"It's not much fun talking to the top or sides of people's heads. Trying to lead worship songs while kids whisper and throw spitballs. Or trying to plan events when half the time there aren't enough people there to warrant using a room as big as our youth room. If I'm not making more of an impact than that, I need to get out of the way and let someone else do it. Someone who's better at it."

"But you're great at it! Is it because I passed that picture around last night?"

"Of course not. That happens every time we're together. You're not the only one who does it."

"But we really are listening. People like me, we're used to doing several things at once. We've always got the TV on, the radio going, the computer beeping. I mean, I can do my homework with Pearl Jam on the radio, 'Saved by the Bell' on television, and three people IM-ing me on the computer. Believe it or not, I really can hear what you're saying when I'm passing notes and pictures."

Gary's face grew somber, and he just watched silently out the windshield as he drove.

"You don't believe me, do you?" Jake asked.

"I believe you, Jake. But I'm not basing my decision on whether you make eye contact with me when I'm talking. I'm going by what you do with your life. If I'm not motivating you into action, into bearing fruit, into caring about other people's lost souls, then I'm not effective as a minister."

"Well, it looks like it's been taken out of your hands. God's making me care about it anyway."

A slow smile crept across Gary's face. "You're right," he said. "It is something only God can do. Sometimes he doesn't need me to do it."

"But *we* need you," Jake said. "If you left now, where would we be?"

"You'd be exactly where you are, only with a new youth minister who might have a little more impact."

Jake didn't like this. "So you're still actually thinking about it? We might run you completely out of the ministry?"

Gary breathed a laugh.

"Come on, you can tell me," Jake said. "I'm not gonna tell anybody. I just want to know if I need to prepare myself."

"I don't know," Gary said. "I'm praying about it."

"So . . . if you thought we were listening, that we were bearing fruit, that we were getting off our duffs and doing some of the stuff you suggested, you think you might stay?"

Gary was noncommittal. "I think I'd be a lot more encouraged. But

I don't want you to do it for me. It's your sole purpose on earth, Jake. Every Christian is supposed to bear fruit, not so the youth minister will feel validated and stay, but because people are drowning all around you and you've got a life preserver."

That analogy kept ringing in Jake's mind as they got to the rehab center and went inside.

Jake didn't know what he had expected in a hospital like this. He had kind of pictured it like those old documentaries of Bedlam—a psychiatric hospital with padded cells and people moaning behind locked doors. What he saw was completely different. The first floor looked like a hospital, with elevators and information booths. When they got off on the second floor, he found that it was designed much like his home. Bright colors gave it a cheery, homey feel. Groupings of couches and chairs sat around television sets, and teenagers and young adults milled around in their own clothes, talking to each other and smiling with their visitors. Against the wall, discreetly placed, was a nurse's desk, and Jake followed Gary to it.

"Yeah, I'd like to see Lou MacLemore, please."

"I'll tell him you're here."

They took their place at a table in the corner, away from the television sets and the talking people. Gary watched the door for the boy to come in, and finally, he saw him. He got to his feet and waved at him, and Lou smiled and crossed the room.

He was a tall boy, way too skinny, and he had dark circles under his eyes. Drugs had really done a number on him. For a moment, Jake felt a little superior that he had never succumbed to the temptation himself. He was too smart for that, he thought. But as Lou approached the table and Gary offered introductions, Jake heard the words coming out of his soul. "I'm starving to death. There's nothing here that can feed me."

He looked at the boy, almost startled, then signaled to Gary that he'd heard. Gary sat them all down at the table. "So how's it going, man?"

Lou shrugged. "Okay, I guess."

"I wanted Jake to come by with me," Gary said, "because I wanted you to get to know some of the kids in my youth group, like we talked about . . ."

"Yeah, okay. Whatever."

"So, are you feeling any better today?" Gary asked.

"Better is relative, isn't it?" Lou asked, nervously rubbing a spot on the table. "They keep me busy. Guess that's good. And it's kind of cool to be able to talk to people who have the same problem."

"How much longer you gonna be in here?" Jake asked.

Lou shot him a surprised look, as if he hadn't expected him to speak. "At least a few more weeks. They want me to have a total attitude adjustment before I leave. Could be a while."

While Lou was talking, Gary was signaling Jake with his eyes to go ahead and blurt out Lou's need. Jake wondered how he wanted him to do it—just tell Lou that he'd heard his soul? He'd tried that once already with Roller-Coaster Rider and it had backfired. He didn't want to be embarrassed again by having his faith thrown in his face. Wasn't there something in the Bible about casting his pearls before swine?

But even as he was rationalizing his silence, he heard the boy's words again. "Nothing's feeding me, and it's eating me alive. Piece by piece."

Suddenly, Jake was ashamed at the thoughts he'd been having. The boy was in agony. He shifted in his seat, and his expression changed as he watched Lou. He prayed a silent prayer that the Lord would tell him what to say and give him the courage to say it. He leaned in and opened his mouth, searching for the right words.

And the right words came.

"You know, Lou, if I were in your place, I think I might feel like I was just starving to death and there wasn't a thing out there that could feed me."

Gary's eyes widened—he understood that Jake was repeating what the Lord had allowed him to hear.

Lou was riveted, listening.

"I think I'd feel like I was being eaten alive," Jake went on.

"You've been through this, haven't you?" Lou asked.

The question surprised Jake. "No, man. I haven't. I was just thinking what it must be like."

The way Lou locked into his gaze, Jake knew he had said exactly the right thing. He wondered if God would keep feeding him the lines like a TelePrompTer if he kept talking. "I've never been addicted to drugs," he said. "And I've never been in rehab. But I've known that hunger."

Still, Lou stared at him, and Jake wondered if, any minute now, Lou would mock him publicly or get up and ask him to leave. For the first time, Jake realized that he might not have very long to talk to the boy, so he decided to get it out. "Two years ago, when I was feeling as hungry as you, my sister told me about someone who could feed me in a way that I'd never been fed before. Someone who could feed me soul food, in the greatest sense of the word. Somebody who could make me stop feeling as if I was being eaten alive."

"Nobody can do that," Lou said.

"Oh, yeah," Jake told him. "Yes, somebody can. Jesus Christ can."

Lou sat back hard in his chair, as if disappointed in the punch line. "I know all about Jesus Christ. I was raised in church. We were there every time the doors opened. I know about Living Water and the Bread of Life and all that, so you're not telling me anything new."

Gary touched Lou's shoulder. "Man, it's one thing to know about Jesus. It's another thing to partake of his power."

Jake held up a hand to stop Gary and met Lou's eyes again. "Man, you don't know Jesus. If you knew Jesus, you would never feel like you were starving to death. You might know all about Jesus, Lou, and you might know more Scripture than I do, which, frankly, wouldn't be that hard. Where Christianity is concerned, I'm pretty pathetic. But I do know Jesus, and I know the power he can give you in your life, and I know the peace that comes from knowing him, even when I'm not very good at being a Christian. If you haven't known that peace, Lou, then maybe you're not really a believer."

"Karl Marx said that religion is the opiate of the masses," the boy said. "I believe him."

Jake looked at Gary, uncertain how to answer that.

"Some people use it as a drug," Gary said. "They hide behind it and under it. Some people use it as a weapon. But it's not supposed to be any of those things, Lou. It's supposed to be something you wear, like a nice warm robe when it's really cold out. You're supposed to 'put on' Christ, like you are him and he is you. You're supposed to let him live inside you, and you're supposed to abide in him. That's the way to abundant life."

"Abundant life," Lou repeated on a whisper. "What a laugh. Everybody in my family goes to church, and none of us has abundant life. We have abundant problems, abundant fights, abundant bills . . ."

"That's because you don't know it's available," Gary said. "If you knew, maybe you could reach out and take it."

As if to distance himself from this conversation, Lou slid his chair back and looked out at the others in the room. His eyes rested on a family sitting around a girl in the corner. "You don't understand," Lou said. "I screwed up. I've done a lot wrong. I don't think God needs somebody like me pulling him down."

"Man, he'll pull you up," Jake said. "He can't be pulled down. He's reaching down to grab your hand and pull you up. Why do you think he sent me here today?"

"Because Gary asked you to come?"

"Well, Gary can ask all he wants," Jake said, "but God put me in a set of circumstances today where I would come, and I could look into your eyes, man, and just know that you need Jesus. And I've gotta ask you. You've tried everything else. Why not give him a chance to change your life? What have you got to lose?"

Tears came to Lou's eyes, and Jake realized he had hit a nerve. The boy rubbed his hands over his face and closed his eyes. Jake looked over at Gary, begging him for help. But Gary smiled and nodded for him to go on. Jake knew that Gary wasn't going to rescue him from this one. It was all in Jake's hands now. All in God's hands.

"Man, I'm just so tired," Lou said, leaning with his elbows on his knees. He rubbed his hands together as he talked. "I'm so tired of fighting. If I could quit drugs that easy, I would. But the problem is, I'll get out of here and I'll go back to my friends, and they'll all be partying and laughing and having a good time, and I'll start thinking about that high from the time I get up in the morning until the time I go to bed at night. It'll be pulling at me. Are you telling me that if I reach out and take something that you think God is offering me, that that won't happen?"

Jake thought that over for a moment. "I'm not sure," he said. "You might still have the cravings. You might still want the drugs. And your friends are still gonna be tugging at you. All I know is that Jesus is the only hope you have."

Lou dropped his face into his chafed hands. "I want that," he said.

"Man, I want that. I want hope. I want something that'll fill me up. I want to try."

Jake glanced at Gary again, trying to pass the baton, but again, Gary wasn't moving.

"What do you want me to do?" Lou asked. "Pray that prayer?"

Jake frowned. "What prayer?"

"Well, at my church, there's always this repeat-after-me kind of thing. That if I say the right formula of words, maybe this time the Holy Spirit will fall over me."

Jake shot Gary a pleading look, but the youth pastor remained silent. "It's not a repeat-after-me kind of thing, Lou. Jesus just wants you to talk to him. He wants you to tell him how hungry you are, how broken. He wants you to tell him all the stuff you've done, that you think he can't forgive you for, and he wants the chance to show you that he can."

"But, man, I'm messed up. God doesn't need somebody like me, somebody who's made such a mess of their lives. He needs people like you."

"Blessed are the poor in spirit," Jake said, "for they shall see God."

Lou looked up at him. "What does that mean?"

Jake was surprised that such a Scripture verse would have come to him in a moment like this. He didn't even know where in the Bible it was found. "I think it means that God blesses the brokenhearted. That when we know how bad off we are, that's when he can work."

"Well, that's where I am," Lou admitted. "I'd be a fool not to see how bad off I am." He laughed through those disturbing tears. "Who am I kidding? I'm a fool."

Jake could feel Lou's pain. He would have done anything to help him. "Man, I'm here with you. Let's pray together. I'll take you to God and introduce you. How about that?"

Lou couldn't speak. He just nodded his head as he bowed it to pray.

seven

Jake knew the meaning of the word "rejoice" as he and Gary headed back to the car. "He gave me the words, Gary," Jake said, practically skipping. "My mind just went blank, and then there they were. The words were just there." He gave the air a victory punch and spun around. "Did you hear him? He asked me to come back! Man, who would have thought?"

Gary was still chuckling as they reached the car, and as they both got in, they began to laugh out loud. Gary leaned his head back on his seat as the laughter played itself out. His smile slowly faded, and he stared out the windshield.

Jake wiped his eyes and tried to catch his breath. "It's amazing. Just amazing."

"Overwhelming," Gary agreed.

Jake snapped his fingers. "That's the word. Overwhelmed. That's what I've been all day!"

Gary kept sitting there, still not moving. "I never thought I'd see that. It was like an answered prayer happening right before my eyes. There you were, Jake Sheffield, leading someone to Christ. Just taking his hand and caring about him, taking him all the way." He looked over at Jake, his face suddenly serious. "Do you realize what you've done?"

Jake's face grew more solemn. "Yeah, I think so."

"And how did it feel?"

"Awesome. Like I was supposed to be doing this all along. Why haven't I?"

"Why haven't you," Gary repeated. "That's a question we should all be asking ourselves. Every one of us." Gary started the car and pulled out of the parking lot.

"I used to think that God's job was to make my life cushy and entertaining and happy," Jake said. "Today I started to realize that it's not about me. God's more interested in his kingdom. In my taking as many people to heaven with me as I can, just like you said. We're here to do something. Man, I wish every Christian could feel like this."

"Maybe this will be contagious," Gary said. "I wouldn't be surprised." He looked at his watch. "Man, I hate it, but I've got to get back to the church. I'm supposed to speak at an elder's dinner tonight."

"No problem," Jake said.

"Look, don't go lock yourself away in the house. Use this high that you're on. Go with it, and see what happens."

"I was thinking I might go back by the mall," Jake said.

Gary looked impressed. "That's a good idea, Jake. Go back to the scene of the crime, and get back on that saddle."

Jake knew his English teacher would have had a field day with the mixed metaphors, but he understood what Gary meant. He couldn't let the humiliation of that morning keep him from going back. There were people there who needed Christ.

The mall was busy this time of day, even busier than the hour just after school, when they had been here earlier. Now people were getting off work and running errands at the mall, cramming as much as they could into daylight. He went to the food court and looked across the crowded tables to the one where the seniors had been sitting earlier today.

Thank you for telling me about Jesus! the guy had yelled, and Jake had wanted to crawl under a table. They had all laughed at him, and he had taken that as a sign that he had no business sharing his faith. But he had been wrong.

His eyes gravitated to Hamburger Haven, where the pregnant girl worked. She was still there, punching orders into the cash register, and throwing wrapped food into paper sacks. Her eyes and nose were red, and he could see that she'd been crying recently. He wished there was something he could do.

For some reason he couldn't quite explain, he went to stand in her line. When he got to the front, she seemed to have a moment of recognition. "Can I help you?"

"Yeah, I'll just have a small Dr. Pepper," he said.

She rang it up, took his money, filled up the cup. As she came back to him, she said, "Uh, listen, I kind of saw what happened today, with you and those guys."

Jake's heart crashed like a water balloon. "Yeah?"

"I just wanted to tell you that I think it was really, really brave. It took a lot of courage to do what you did. To tell somebody about Jesus, even when you knew you could be mocked. I'm sorry they did that."

He smiled. Was this God's way of telling him that he had done the right thing to come back? Was God urging him to talk to *her?* "Thanks, I appreciate that."

A long line had formed behind him, so he got his drink and headed to a table, sat down, and looked back at her. Another worker had approached her and was taking over the cash register. He watched the girl take off her apron and the little hat with the Hamburger Haven emblem on the front. *She must be getting off of work*, he thought. He prayed a silent prayer that the Lord would give him the chance to talk to her again. Things weren't settled with her. Not by a long shot.

She went to the back, then emerged with her purse. Jake stood up as she came around the counter. He didn't know what he was going to say to her, but his urgency was greater than his fear. "Excuse me," he said. "Beth Ann, right?"

She stopped. "Yeah?"

"I was wondering if you were okay. My youth minister was talking to you today, and I could tell you were upset."

She swallowed and looked away. "Yeah, I'm okay."

"You wanna talk about it? I don't have anyplace to go for a while."

She looked up at him for a moment, and those tears shimmered in her eyes again. "I guess so. Why not?"

She took the seat across from him and set her elbows on the table. "Are you gonna talk to me about Jesus too?" she asked with a sad smile.

"If you'll listen."

"Because, if it's just a come-on, you should know that I'm probably not a person you'd want to get involved with right now."

He knew Beth Ann was referring to her pregnancy, and he didn't want to add insult to injury by telling her he wasn't interested. But he desperately wanted her to take him seriously. "It's not a come-on," he said.

She was a pretty girl, even with red eyes. He wondered what she would look like with her face lit up in a smile and peace in her eyes. "Did your youth minister tell you what my problem is?"

No, I told him. Jake knew he couldn't be that blunt, but he didn't quite know where to go from there. "Gary keeps private conversations to himself. That's why he's good to talk to."

"Well . . ." She gave an exhausted sigh. "Since I don't even know you and may not ever see you again, I might as well tell you, because I really do need to talk about it." She looked down at the table. "See, I'm pregnant."

She let the word hang there, like a spider web woven between them, and watched to see if he would swat it away or just peer through it.

"How do you feel about that?" he asked.

She breathed a humorless laugh. "I feel pretty scared. I haven't been able to tell my boyfriend, because ever since I mentioned that I thought I might be, he's made himself scarce, and I'm thinking about getting an abortion, but your youth pastor tried to talk me out of it, and I don't know what I'm gonna do. I just know that I've never been so out of control in my life, and I don't like this feeling, and I don't know where to turn. So . . ." She dropped her palms on the table and drew in a deep breath. "So, if you have anything to tell me about Jesus or how he can solve these problems, I'd kind of like to hear it right now. 'Cause it looks to me like there's no way out that's acceptable, and either way, I've ruined my life."

"You haven't ruined your life," Jake said. "You've got way too much life ahead of you. Have you tried just giving it to God?"

"Not yet," she said. "Would I suddenly not be pregnant anymore and not have to make a decision about nine months of humiliation . . . or abortion or adoption?"

"No," he said. "You'll still have to deal with those decisions. But God can make them with you. He can walk through it with you."

She laughed out loud, shaking her head. "See, I've never understood that about God walking with me. You Christians always talk like that, but I don't know what it means. I mean, do you see him walking beside you? Like a ghost or something?"

"No, of course not," Jake said. "It's the spirit of him inside of us. We don't have to be without him."

"But does he want to walk with some girl who's pregnant and not married? Some girl who's messed up her life by giving herself to a boy who couldn't care less?"

"Yes, Beth Ann," he said without hesitation. "That's just the kind of person Jesus wants."

She looked at him quietly for a long moment, letting his words sink in. "So how come you're going around today telling people about Jesus?"

He thought of telling her the truth but knew she would think he was mentally ill. "Let's just say I started listening to the Holy Spirit. He made me realize there are people hurting. But it doesn't have to be that way, you know? There's something I know, something I can tell them."

"You know, if I were to become a Christian now, it would really limit my choices."

"How do you figure that?"

"Well, if I became a Christian, I'd have to rule out abortion. Thou shalt not kill, right? 'Course, some people don't think abortion is murder . . . Maybe they're just not being honest with themselves; I don't know. Maybe they just want the convenient way out. I sure do."

He couldn't answer that. There had been a time when he'd considered himself wise enough to debate on any and every subject. But today he'd learned how much he didn't know.

"But I need to keep my options open. I have a right to decide what to do with my body."

"That's between you and God," Jake said. "All I know is that knowing Jesus has given me more choices, not less. Sometimes when we choose our own path, we find ourselves more imprisoned, not free. Today I've seen a lot of people trapped in their own prisons. I've never felt like I was in a prison. At least, not since I've known Jesus."

"That's a good word for it," she said. "Prison."

"If you become a Christian, you're gonna see things differently. It's not that God's taking away your choices. It's just that he's clarifying them. You'll see in a way that you didn't see before."

"I don't know," she said. "I know a lot of Christians who don't see anything differently. They make the same choices and seem to believe in the same things when it comes right down to it. They're hypocrites. They say one thing but do something else."

"You can't measure your life by what other people do," he said. "All you can do is have a relationship with Christ and let him tell you what to do. God doesn't handcuff us and make us do what he wants. He always gives us choices."

"It's hard to live a Christian life, though," she said. "You have to give up so much."

"The things that you give up are the things that are hurting and imprisoning you," he said. "What you get instead is someone who loves you enough to die for you. The person who created you. The person who knows you better than you know yourself and who knows just what you need."

Beth Ann looked down at her hands. "You seem like an honest guy," she said. "Like you really believe all this."

"I do."

"But you can't know for sure if you're right."

"I am sure," he said, leaning in until she looked up at him again. "I'm absolutely positive."

"But how? How can you know?"

"Because I have abundant life," he said. "And I haven't even tapped into all the things the Holy Spirit has for me. Until today, I didn't even know all the power I have to rescue people's souls, to keep them from drowning."

The words seemed to strike a chord within her, and Jake got that feeling that the Lord had done it again. He had given Jake the words. He had reached inside of Beth Ann and gotten her attention. "I don't want to drown," she whispered as she gazed at him.

"I don't want you to drown, either," he said. "And I don't want you to try to swim when you can't even see the shore. Why don't you take hold of this life preserver I'm throwing you? Let the Lord pull you in."

All the exhaustion and despair and shame seemed to pull at her face at the same time as big tears spilled down her cheek. "Just tell me how."

eight

When Jake got home, Heather was there, standing in front of the refrigerator and staring at the contents, like something would reach out and grab her hand and tell her that was what she was to eat that afternoon. Eating was always a major decision for Heather. She felt as if she had to stay lean to be a good swimmer. Jake felt that swimming made her lean, and she didn't need to worry so much about what she ate.

Still, she just stood there, letting all the cold air out into the room.

"Hey, sis."

"Where have you been?" she asked, giving him a cursory glance. "Mom said you came home from school today. You don't look sick to me."

He was bursting to tell someone other than Gary what had happened to him, but he knew most people would think he had gone over the edge. Word would travel quickly that he had snapped. His sister, on the other hand, would keep it quiet, if only for her own reputation. "You're not gonna believe what's happened," he said.

"Tell me," she said, then showed a decided lack of interest in Jake's story by turning back to the refrigerator. He stepped up beside her and reached in for an apple, put it in her hand, then closed the door. She looked down at it, then shrugged and bit into it.

"So what happened?" she asked with her mouth full.

"Heather, do you remember this morning when I got up early before you went to swim team?"

"Yeah," she said. "You couldn't sleep." Actually, it sounded like "Yeyucunswp." But he knew what she meant.

"That's right. Do you remember the dream I told you about?"

Thankfully, she swallowed this time before she spoke. "Yeah. Did it come true?"

"No, no! Just listen. Did I tell you about the voice I thought was God's—it said a word?"

"I don't know."

"Well, the word was *Ephphatha*. I talked to Gary and we looked it up, and it's in the Bible, Heather!"

"Yeah? So? Lots of words are in the Bible." She wasn't getting it.

"But it's the passage where they bring a deaf man to Christ, and he spits on his fingers and puts them in the man's ears and says, 'Ephphatha! Be opened.' And instantly the man is able to speak and hear."

Heather took another bite of the apple. "Uh-huh?"

"Well, that was in my dream. It *was* God speaking to me. I really did hear his voice."

She pulled a barstool back from the counter and slid onto it. "Thought you said it was something you ate last night."

"No, just listen," he said. "I went to the school library this morning to work on my term paper, and I started hearing these voices. People were talking, only they weren't saying anything."

"That's why I never study in the library," she said. "I can't hear myself think in there."

"I heard them saying things they weren't really saying, Heather. Like one person said he was a loser, and another one said he was in a dark tunnel and couldn't find any light."

"People said these things to you?"

"No, they didn't say it out loud. They thought it or felt it or their soul cried it out—I don't know. All I know is that I had that dream this morning, and I heard God speaking, and the next thing I know, I'm hearing things people are not saying!"

He had her attention now, but instead of looking impressed, she looked slightly afraid. She slowly got up from the table and inched toward the telephone.

"What are you doing? I'm talking to you."

"I have to call mom," she said. "She wanted a report when you got home, since you weren't feeling well."

"So what are you gonna tell her? That I'm talking crazy?" She started to dial, and he crossed the room and stopped her. "Heather, don't."

"You're scaring me," she said.

"Don't be scared. Just listen. Heather, I led two people to Christ today. Two people, can you believe that? And because I was able to tell Gary what people were thinking, *he* was able to lead some too."

"You told Gary about this?"

"Yes! That's who I've been with most of the afternoon. And he believed me and went with me, and he was able to talk to people and meet them right there at need level."

"Knee level?" she asked.

"Need level. Heather, you're not listening."

"I want to be useful like that."

He heard the words, but her mouth didn't move. "There you go! You just said you want to be useful like that! You thought it, didn't you?"

Heather looked startled.

"In fact, you said it this morning. Remember, at breakfast? I heard you say that you wanted to catch some fish."

Her eyebrows were coming together as she tried to absorb what he was saying.

"Heather, just sit down and take a few deep breaths. I know I heard what you were thinking. If you'll just sit down and think about it, you'll realize that's one of your needs. You may not know it, but . . . That's what I've found out today; sometimes people aren't aware of their needs."

She looked at him out of the corner of her spooked eyes. "How do you know you're not just hallucinating, then, if they don't know they thought it?"

Frustrated, he dropped his hands. "I should have known you wouldn't buy it. I mean, who would, really? But it doesn't matter. It's happened. I led two people to Christ today and planted a dozen other seeds, and it was so cool, you just wouldn't believe it. I mean, it's like I have this power I didn't know I had. The power to rescue people and tell them things that'll save their lives."

Now she was listening with less fear in her eyes. He sat down again.

"Heather, I went to the rehab center with Gary and saw this guy he's been visiting. I told him about Jesus. He was crying, Heather, and he wound up praying and asking Christ to come into his heart. It was the coolest thing."

"You did that?" she asked. "Really?"

"Yes!"

"I want offspring of my own," her heart said.

Jake practically jumped and pointed at her. "There you go. I heard it again. You said you want offspring." He frowned. "What do you mean you want offspring?"

Now her eyes were widening, and she got up and backed away. "You heard that?"

"Yes, I told you!"

"I mean, I've just been thinking that I've never led that many people to Christ."

"You led me," he said.

"Yeah, you," she said, as if that didn't count. "But I mean anybody else. And I've been thinking, I want to have Christian offspring, be fruitful and multiply."

"Oh, I get it."

"And you *heard* me say that?"

"Yes," he said. "You've got to listen to me, Heather. I'm not making this up. God opened my ears and I can hear what he hears. It's like I have a peek inside people's souls."

She gaped at him, her mouth hanging open. "This is weird," she said. She looked at the phone again. "Do you think I should call mom?"

"No," he said. "She's got enough problems right now. I don't want to worry her. She might not be able to deal with it. I just had to tell somebody besides Gary. At first, today, when I figured it out, I was really upset because I didn't want it. I felt like God was punishing me for being lukewarm or something. But Gary showed me that it's a gift, and I don't know why he gave it to me, Heather, but he did, and it's the coolest thing because I can lead people to Christ, and you just don't know what that feels like!"

Her eyes were brightening. "I want to hear it," she said. "I want to go with you and see what it's like. I want you to tell me what you hear."

"Okay," he said. "I'm up for it if you are."

She took another bite of her apple, obviously considering the situation as she chewed. "The ball game tonight," she said. "You can come with me and tell me things about all my friends. Hey! Tell me if Brianne really likes Ted Nelson, because she says she doesn't, but I sense a real strong chemistry there—"

"I don't have much choice in what I hear. I can't just zoom into people's thoughts. And I don't know if I really want to be seen with my sister at the ball game tonight. What will people think?"

"I promise I won't show them pictures of you as a naked baby, okay? I just want to see how this works."

"Trust me, Heather. It works."

"Well, why you? Why not somebody more . . ."

"Equipped?" he asked.

"Yeah, that's the word."

"That's the question I've been asking all day. But he did choose me, and I'm starting to be excited about it." He swallowed hard. "Imagine what he has planned for my life, to give me a gift like this."

"But you don't even know that much Scripture. You're, like, the worst person I could think of."

"Thanks, Sis, I can always count on you to be honest with me. Not to mention encouraging."

"I'm not trying to hurt your feelings, Jake. I just don't get it."

"I don't know, maybe God was trying to light a fire under me," he said. "But whatever the case, he's taught me today that all I really need to know is what Jesus did for me and what he can do for others."

Heather's eyes twinkled with amusement as she stared at her brother. "I never thought I'd hear you talk like this," she said. "That, in itself, is a miracle."

He shook his head and grinned. "Heather, you ain't seen nothing yet."

nine

The ball game had already started when Jake and Heather got there. Andy and Logan waited for Jake just inside the gate. "Man, where have you been?" Andy asked. "Kick-off was ten minutes ago. We've got the ball."

Jake glanced at the field, but he was too distracted to care about the game.

"Come on," Andy said. "Let's sit down."

Jake looked back over his shoulder and saw that Heather had met up with her friends. Trina Bradshaw was among them, and he found his heart skipping a beat. There were advantages to hanging out with his sister, he thought.

"Get a row with enough room for Heather and her fan club," he said. "She's stuck to me tonight."

"Why?" Andy demanded.

"It's sort of . . . a dare," he said, knowing that wouldn't need much more explanation. "Just find an empty row."

He glanced back and saw Heather trying to herd her group along as he started toward the bleachers.

"Everything works out wrong, and chance is always against me." Jake stopped when he heard the words, and he turned into the crowd and tried to zero in on the voice. There were too many people around, pushing through the bottleneck at the bottom of the student section.

He looked up and realized Andy and Logan were already halfway up. Quickly, he followed them and took a seat. Heather and six of her closest friends squeezed past them to sit down. As Trina Bradshaw passed, he heard her voice, as clear as if it was whispering in his ear.

"I'm so ugly. If they could see past my face they'd know. *Abused* is such a clinical word for ugliness like mine."

He looked up at her, startled. He could use such information, he thought. It could give him definite inroads in getting her to go out with him. If he could make her feel pretty on the inside . . .

Then just as quickly as the thoughts had come, he mentally kicked himself. What was he thinking? She'd said the word *abuse,* and all he could think of was himself.

She looked down at him, as if wondering why he was staring at her.

"You look nice tonight, Trina," he said.

She rolled her eyes and took her seat. "Thanks."

He felt like an idiot, but the desire to make her feel better was overwhelming. As the other girls filed in on the other side of her, he leaned toward her. "I meant on the inside."

She frowned. "Huh?"

He was making it worse, he thought. She didn't seem to know what he was talking about.

"Grange is gonna make it!" Logan shouted, springing to his feet. "Look at that. Next play is a sure touchdown!"

The band, which was seated in the section next to them, started playing, creating more havoc, and the cheerleaders led a chorus of chaos. Trina's eyes fixed on his, as if she was searching their depths for the meaning of his words. He had her, he thought with a thrill of triumph. He had a telescope into her soul. If that didn't give him an advantage over those seniors she usually dated, he didn't know what would.

Heather plopped down between them, breaking the connection. He leaned forward and tried to catch Trina's eyes again, but she was looking down at the field.

He had done it again, he thought, hating himself. God hadn't told him Trina's deepest needs so that Jake could score points with her.

He made himself sick.

Then the voices started again. "I've got to leave, get away, disappear so no one will ever see me again."

He felt the desperate plea from the bottom of someone's soul. He thought it was the girl in front of him, but she didn't look like she was going anywhere.

"They don't even know it'll soon be over," another voice interrupted.

Jake turned around and saw Zeke, the Goth who'd run into him in the library earlier, with a video camera against his eye. He was taping the crowd, not the game. He didn't seem to be the sentimental type, so Jake wondered why he'd be recording the faces of people he didn't seem to like.

Then a cacophony of voices started in.

"If one person in the world could love me . . ."

"I don't know how I'll ever belong."

"What if they know what I've done?"

"I'm sinking, sinking, sinking."

Jake was beginning to feel sick, and the voices were getting louder, along with the audible shouting as Grange dropped the ball and the other team recovered it. The band played faster and harder, and those cheerleaders screeched into megaphones below, "Go Franklin High!"

Jake got to his feet. "I've got to get out of here," he told Heather.

She looked up at him. "Jake, you're sweating. Are you okay?"

"No. Uh . . . I've got a headache." He leaned over to her. "The voices are everywhere. I can't stay here."

"You want me to get you a drink? Or maybe a mental-health professional?"

"Heather, this is not funny!"

"Okay, okay." She got up. "I'll go with you."

He nodded and started out of the row.

"Where ya going, man?" Logan asked him. "Are you having a family conference or something?"

"I've got a headache." He tripped over Andy's leg.

"What's the hurry, man?" Andy asked. "Jake, what's the matter?"

"Headache," he said. "I'll be back later."

He got out of the row and headed down the aisle, with Heather fast on his heels.

"Jake, are you sure you're all right? You're shaking."

"It was a nightmare," he said. "They were all talking to me, everybody around me. I just have to get somewhere where there aren't any crowds. Maybe the concession area."

"What did you hear? Were any of them my friends?"

"Yeah, Trina," he said, still walking fast as he pushed through the cluster of people at the edge of the bleachers. "Heather, if I tell you this, you have to promise not to tell anybody. I'm only telling you because . . . well, maybe you can help her. My motives aren't pure. I've wanted to go out with her since the ninth grade."

"You have? Trina? *Really?*"

"Yes. But she needs to know the Lord, Heather. She thinks she's ugly on the inside, and I think it has something to do with some abuse . . . maybe at home. That's why she's always so worried about her looks. She thinks if people look past her exterior, they'll see the ugliness. She needs to know that the Lord looks inside her and sees a scared, beautiful little girl. She needs to know she's a princess."

"A princess?"

"The child of a King. You know, joint heirs with Christ? Except I can't tell her, because I'm not sure if I'd be doing it for Christ's kingdom or for my love life."

"Right," she said, trying to follow him. "I'll talk to her, Jake. Tonight, after the game."

They reached the concession area, but there was a crowd around the stand. Jake couldn't bear to go closer. He slowed to a stop and realized he was sweating like a horse. "I just want to stand here a minute," he said. "Would you get me a drink?"

"Sure, but I'm not using my own money. You'll have to pay—"

He reached into his pocket and thrust a dollar at her. "There, okay? A bottled water. Just . . . hurry. I feel like I might pass out."

She hurried to the concession stand and waited patiently in line. Heaven forbid that, just this once, she should explain to someone that her brother was on the verge of passing out and needed water to keep from collapsing. No, Heather had to stand there and wait her turn like she had all the time in the world.

After an eternity, she brought him the bottled water, and he gulped half of it down in one drink. "Thanks," he said.

"So are you gonna show me here?"

He wiped his brow and looked down at her. "Show you what?"

"This power you have. Are you going to show me?"

He closed his eyes as a group of kids walked by. "I don't know, Heather. I just don't feel—"

"I have those pills. I could take them all at once. They'd miss me then."

He stood straighter and looked at the girl whose voice he'd heard. It was Cela Henderson, the homecoming queen. He couldn't believe such a thought had come from her soul, when she was smiling and chattering as if everything was fine.

"Cela," he whispered to his sister. "She's thinking of suicide."

"No way," Heather said. "Not her. She's too stuck on herself."

"Yes, her. Heather, you've got to get past the way things appear. They're not like that at all. Come on." He started toward the girl, cutting through her entourage. "Cela!"

The class beauty turned around, still smiling. "Hi, Jake."

"Cela, can I talk to you? It's real important."

"Can it wait?" she asked. "I'm looking for somebody."

"No, it can't wait." He stepped closer and lowered his voice. "It's about . . . those pills you have."

Heather didn't gasp, but she might as well have. Her mouth was wide open. Cela stopped cold. Her smile faded, and she looked at her friends and said, "Go on, I'll catch up."

Her friends left her, and she came face to face with Jake. "What are you talking about, Jake?"

He swallowed. At least he had gotten her attention. "Cela, I know this sounds insane, but the Lord just revealed to me that you're contemplating suicide, and I think the fact that I know just goes to show you how much he loves you and wants you to—"

"I haven't told anyone," she said. "How did you know?"

Heather's eyes grew wider, and she looked up at her brother, waiting.

"I told you. The Lord revealed it to me, and I can't say how, because it really doesn't make a whole lot of sense, but then, lots of things that don't make sense to us make sense to God."

Tears filled her eyes almost instantly, and her mouth began to tremble. "I can't believe—"

"Cela, you think no one cares about you, but the Lord cares so much that he brought me right here to this spot to tell you he wants you to know what he did for you and what that can mean in your life. He wants you to know that Jesus Christ wants you in his family, that you can have eternal life and abundant life. And you don't want to cut it short."

She started to cry and looked nervously from side to side and covered her face with her hands. "He really told you about me?"

"Yes, Cela. You're so special to him. Special enough to die for."

"But you don't know what I'm really like."

"He does. He wants you anyway, Cela. No matter what you've done. No matter who you've been."

She looked from him to Heather and back. "Do you know . . . about me . . . the things I've done?"

He had heard rumors, but he didn't know any of them to be true. "No, Cela. I guess God didn't need for me to know that. He just told me enough to give me the courage to talk to you."

She swallowed and looked down at her feet, still crying. "What an awesome thing."

"What?" he asked.

"For God to care that much about a person. For him to care about me." She looked up at him. "You really think I could be a Christian, with all the stuff in my life?"

"I know you could. He wants you just like you are. He can clean you up. He did me, didn't he, Heather?"

Heather was still staring at Cela. "Uh . . . yes. I mean . . . boy, did he. You should have seen him. He was a real jerk, and he had a foul mouth, and he used to smart off to my mom all the time and insult me every time he breathed and—"

"Thanks, Heather," Jake cut in. "I think she gets the point. But, Cela, you can see that God doesn't wait until you've cleaned up your act. He wants you now. Just like you are. When you turn your life over to him, he'll give you his Holy Spirit, so you don't have to clean up your act all on your own. He helps you, Cela. He stays with you. And you know what? You'll never wish you were dead again."

She breathed in a sob. "I want that."

"Then let me pray for you," he said. "And then you can tell God."

Heather reached for Cela's hand, and Jake took her other one. They were wet with her tears.

"Cela!" One of her friends yelled from the concession stand.

She turned around and nodded that she was coming. That was it, Jake thought. They'd lost her. She would run off now and shake free of the convictions he'd stirred. She would forget it until she looked at that bottle of pills.

"She can wait," Cela whispered. "I want to pray."

Heather did gasp this time and smiled up at Jake with shock on her face. Jake's heart soared. He closed his eyes and began to pray.

ten

When Cela had returned to her friends, Heather looked at him as if he'd just turned water to wine. "That's the coolest thing I've ever seen."

"I told you."

"You hit the nail on the head. You said exactly the right stuff."

"It wasn't me it was God," he said. "He told me exactly the right words. And the things I told her were just what I already knew to be true about Jesus. Things *you* told me."

"Do it again," she said.

"I can't do it on command. I'm not telepathic."

But even as he spoke, a group of Goths strode by, all dressed in black, with dyed black hair and black eye make-up. One of the guys had a tattoo of a snake that ran down his jaw.

"I'm in too deep. Can't get out. It's too late." Jake heard the words from the one with the snake.

"Do you know that guy?" he asked.

"Yeah, it's Viper. He's a senior. I'm scared of him."

"Well, I'm not. I'm going to talk to him."

"Be prepared. He'll insult you. He might even hurt you. They walk around daring people to cross them."

"God let me hear his need. If God cares, I can care."

A group of sophomore girls came by, and Jake heard another voice. "I can't live without him. Nobody on this planet loves me. Not one single soul."

Jake stopped and turned back to Heather. "That girl right there, with the blue streak in her hair. She thinks nobody loves her. Go tell her who does."

Heather looked startled. "Jake, I don't know. You're the one who heard."

"I have to talk to that Viper person. Go ahead, Heather. Somebody has to tell her before she gets away."

Heather looked as if she was heading to the gas chamber as she cut across the dirt and began to speak to the girl.

Viper wasn't about to talk seriously with Jake in front of his friends, let alone accept Christ, but Jake managed to tell him that he wasn't in too deep, that it wasn't too late, that Jesus Christ paid the price for whatever Viper had done, and that he would be available to talk later if Viper needed to talk. He gave him one of Gary's cards with the church's address on it and invited him to church on Sunday. The kid looked totally uninterested, but he didn't throw the card away. Jake saw him slide it into his pocket.

When the Goths had threaded back into the crowd, Jake looked around for Heather. She and the blue-streaked girl were under the bleachers, sitting on one of the bleacher's support bars as Heather talked to her. The girl was riveted on her, and he could tell that Heather was speaking from her heart. "You go, girl," he whispered.

"Jake! Where have you been?"

He swung around and saw Andy. "Oh, Andy, you're not gonna believe what's happening. I've been down here telling people about Jesus, man, and some of them are listening. A girl—I can't tell you her name— was about to kill herself, but I led her to Christ. And there was a guy—"

"Man, Grange just fumbled the ball again, but then he recovered it and ran it almost to the end zone. You gotta see this."

"We're all fumbling the ball," Jake said. "Don't you see, man? We Christians are fumbling all over the place. But today I recovered the ball, and I've spent the whole day talking to people about Jesus, and, man, it's the greatest thing in the world. Greater than your team winning the Super Bowl. Better than *playing* in the Super Bowl!"

"You don't know what it's like to play in the Super Bowl."

"I'm trying to make a point. Why don't you stay here and talk to people with me? You'll see how great it is."

"Man, we could still win. I came to see the game."

"But there are hurting people all around us, Andy. We're here for a purpose."

"Yeah, to watch the game. Man, what is wrong with you?"

Jake's excitement crashed as he realized he wasn't going to get through to his friend.

"I can't be used." The voice came from nowhere, and yet he knew it was Andy's.

"You can be used, Andy. You can. I didn't think I could, but I have. Just try it."

Andy shook his head and started to walk away. "I'm getting a soda. Man, come on back with me. Watch the game."

"I'm not a spectator anymore," Jake said. "I can't sit there with all those hurting souls around me."

"Yeah, okay. Whatever." Shaking his head as if he didn't know what to think of Jake's new passion, Andy headed for the concession stand.

Jake felt as though he'd blown it, but he turned back to Heather and remembered what this was all about. He saw Heather writing something—he guessed it was her phone number—on the girl's hand, then hug her. She had done it, he thought. She had led the girl to Christ. Man, that was worth whatever Andy thought about him.

The girl came out from under the bleachers, her eyes glowing with tears as she made her way back to the stands. Heather followed, grinning from ear to ear, as she approached Jake. "Did you see that? Did you see it? Jake, she listened to me! She really listened! Isn't that awesome?"

"I told you."

"Let's do it again," Heather said. "I'll take the next one that comes along, and you take the one after that. Just tell me what you hear. Jake, do you realize what you have? Do you realize it?"

Jake laughed at that very realization as he waited for the next voice.

eleven

A fter the game, Jake and Heather went their separate ways, and Jake caught up to his friends. They had lost the game, and everyone was brooding. But Jake couldn't even pretend to be depressed.

"You should have seen it," Logan told him. "Grange must have had lard on his fingers. He was fumbling the ball all over the place."

"Don't be so hard on him," Jake said. "The guy is terrified of being a loser. I think his father must put a lot of pressure on him. There's no telling how torn up he is about it."

Logan shot him a look. "I never got that impression. He's so cocky you'd think he couldn't lose if he tried."

"It's just a facade," Jake said. "Trust me. Inside of that guy, there's nothing but turmoil."

Logan looked at Andy, and they both burst out laughing. "Right," Andy said. "Poor Grange. He's concrete on the outside and pudding on the inside. What are you, Jake? His shrink?"

"No, I just . . . get the feeling."

"So, why did you disappear on us?" Logan asked, though Jake suspected that Andy had already told him what he'd been doing.

"Heather and I decided to try witnessing to some people," he said. "We might have headed off a suicide tonight, and we led at least two people to Christ."

Andy slid his hands into his pockets and shook his head. "Give me a break."

"What do you mean?"

"Do you really believe that a person can pray a prayer at a football game and be sincere about it? I don't."

"People need to hear, Andy. I can't refuse to tell them just because of where they are. Their salvation is between them and God. I'm just a messenger with information they need. God can work anywhere. You should have seen the Goth I talked to. There was this one with a snake tattooed on his face—"

"Viper?" Logan asked.

"Yeah. I talked to him. I mean, he didn't convert or anything, but he took my phone number and didn't throw it away. I think a seed might have been planted."

Logan gaped at him as if he'd lost his mind. "Jake, what's gotten into you?"

"What?"

They reached the parking lot and threaded their way through the cars. "Witnessing to Viper? What did you do? Stand there and look for, like, the most dangerous person at our school?"

"He's not dangerous. He's depressed. He's gotten into some things that he can't quite get out of. He's a person, guys. Christ died for him."

"Did he laugh at you?"

Jake got into the backseat as they took the front. "No, he didn't laugh. But even if he had, I would have done it. I got laughed at today at the food court in the mall. I wanted to crawl under a table. But the more I think about it, the more I realize that Christ took a whole lot more than ridicule on that cross. If the worst thing that ever happens to me is a little embarrassment . . . well, I can live with that."

Andy pulled out of the parking lot. "So, where do you guys wanna go?"

"Pizza Hut," Logan said.

"That's fine," Jake said. "Guys, we're all Christians here. God didn't leave us here just to get comfortable and stagnant. He wanted us to *do* something. Our main purpose is to tell as many people as we can about Jesus. Why aren't we doing that?"

"People know I'm a Christian," Logan said. "I'm president of Fellowship of Christian Athletes. During baseball season, I'm the one who leads the team in prayer. Last year, whenever I hit a home run, I would kneel at home plate and pray. People see that, Jake. It's worth something."

"It's great," Jake said. "And, man, when you do that . . . I'm so proud. But it's one thing to take a public stand like that and another to talk to the little nerd guy who sits next to you in science. Or the girl standing behind you in the lunch line. Or a teacher whose husband has left her, and she needs to know what we know."

Logan stared back at him with his mouth open. "Who are you?"

Andy cracked up, and Jake sat back, grinning. "Okay, I deserved that. I don't even like to be called on to pray in Sunday school. I've never dropped to my knees after making it to base, at least not on purpose."

Again, they snickered.

"And you couldn't have forced me to walk up to somebody and start telling them about Jesus. Man, you should have seen me this morning when all this started."

"That's what I don't get," Andy said. "What happened this morning? You were weird when you came out of the library."

Jake thought of telling them but decided it was a sure way to lose friends. "I wasn't feeling well at school, so I went to see Gary—"

"Gary? You always go to Gary when you're sick?"

"I wasn't sick, okay?" Jake said. "Just kind of depressed. And we got to talking about the impact he was having on us, or the lack of impact, and he kind of challenged me to go out with him today and witness to people."

"You played hooky from school so you could witness to people?" Andy was amused.

"I was not playing hooky. I really felt bad. And it wasn't until after school hours that we went to the mall and talked to people in the food court and the arcade, and I watched Gary lead some people to Christ, and then I talked to that guy behind the counter at the arcade. You know, black guy, goes to our school too?"

"That guy who's always mad? Why did you wanna talk to him?"

Jake wanted to tell them that the Lord had revealed L. J.'s need to him today, that he was just responding. "Same reason I talked to anybody. They all have needs, okay? Some of them are hurting."

"People like him and that Viper guy are major-league losers," Andy said. "Which reminds me. Did you see that Zeke guy behind us with the video camera at the game? What's he doing? Making a documentary about school spirit?"

Logan laughed. "Yeah, Zeke's always been real interested in school spirit. Give him a megaphone and a switchblade, and he can get people yelling, all right."

"You've got him wrong," Jake said. "He needs the Lord. Imagine if we were all out telling people what the Lord has done for us—one by one—we'd lead everybody in our school to Christ. There would never be a need for school security systems or metal detectors."

"Oh, so it's our fault that some people are evil?" Logan asked.

"No, of course not. But it may be our fault that they haven't found what's good."

They pulled into the Pizza Hut parking lot, and he could see as they got out that his friends were getting a little aggravated at him. He needed to back off, he thought.

But he wasn't sure that was an option.

Pizza Hut was already full of kids from the game, and Jake and his friends pushed through the crowd, greeting some and insulting others as they went.

Jake was distracted as they made their way to the table, for already he was hearing voices.

"I hate myself. Everybody else hates me."

"If I could just get skinny I'd finally be happy."

"I said all the wrong things tonight. I'm such a loser."

He tried to ignore them as they pushed through and found one of the few empty tables. It was covered with food and dishes from the previous customers, so the guys began to stack things precariously and move them to another table. When they'd gotten down to the sticky surface, they slid into the booth.

"If someone would just listen."

He heard the male voice behind him, and he turned to see Sheree Jones with her boyfriend, H. R. Blythe, who was running his mouth off, as usual. She looked interested, as interested as anyone could be when H. R. Blythe was talking about his theory about the wind. He had reinvented the wheel—er, the wind—and thought he'd come up with some fascinating concepts about meteorology and the earth's gravitational pull. Jake thought he was one of those people no one would take seriously in high school, but some time later he would become another Bill Gates and be the most fascinating guy at the twenty-year reunion.

That voice couldn't have come from him, Jake thought. H. R. believed everyone was listening, which was why he never stopped talking.

"No one hears me. I'm uninteresting and boring. Nothing but an aggravation to everyone who knows me."

No mistake. The voice had definitely come from him. Jake thought of sliding out of the booth to talk to the guy, but Andy had him blocked in.

"I need help planning the prayer breakfast for Friday," Logan said. "I was gonna feature a different youth pastor from churches around here every week, but the one at Mount Sinai quit last week, so I'm left holding the bag. Any ideas for who could come?"

"Man, we're talking breakfast at McDonald's," Andy said. "We don't need a speaker."

"But if we don't have one, then it's chaos. There's not really a purpose for it."

"People will still come," Andy said, "just because they like Egg McMuffins." He took a big gulp of his drink.

Jake tried to focus on the conversation. "I'll speak."

Andy choked on his drink, and Logan cracked up.

"No, I'm serious. I'll talk about what I've been telling you tonight. About our purpose for being here. About our sharing Christ."

"No offense, but that isn't exactly the place for such a heavy subject."

"A prayer breakfast isn't the place?"

Andy blew off his paper straw cover, and it sailed over Jake's head. "He means McDonald's. It's kind of a light place, and all of our speakers in the past have just sort of given a feel-good devotion or something."

"Then let's change it. Let's see if Gary will open the church for it."

"Man, no one will come to the church," Andy said. "They don't have food!"

He was getting the message. His friends didn't want him to speak. He couldn't blame them, he realized. Until tonight, he'd been just another self-indulgent, lukewarm Christian who didn't have a clue what God wanted of him. He turned his palms up. "Okay, then you come up with somebody."

"I know," Andy said. "What about Trina Bradshaw? She could do a cool devotion."

Jake couldn't believe his ears. "Trina? Why? She's not even a Christian."

"Of course, she's a Christian. She's a member of FCA, isn't she? Besides, she's cute to look at, and I like her voice."

"Oh, great. That's what you're looking for in a prayer breakfast speaker? Cute?"

Logan snorted. "He's just jealous because he's been salivating after her for years."

"I have not," Jake said. "Don't be so crude."

Again, Andy and Logan cracked up. "That's it," Logan said. "It's official. An alien has inhabited Jake's body. This guy is an impostor."

Jake didn't find his friends' laughter amusing, and he slammed his hand on the table. "What is wrong with you guys? Look around you. Most of the people in this room are lost. You should hear what goes on in their souls! They're just crying out for help, and here we sit talking about Trina Bradshaw and Egg McMuffins! What do you think God thinks about all this?"

"Hey, God made Trina *and* Egg McMuffins," Logan said, and they both cracked up again.

"I want to be righteous." The words came as naturally from Logan's soul as the chortles that came from his mouth.

"I'm no help to God."

Jake looked at Andy, who was still snickering, and realized that his soul was crying out too.

"If only I could make a difference." Logan was muttering something about Trina Bradshaw again, but Jake heard differently.

The Holy Spirit inside them was crying out to bear fruit. But they wouldn't listen.

A flurry of activity near the door snagged their attention, and he saw Grange and several of the football players coming in with their letter jackets, even though it wasn't cold enough out for a jacket. They had

I-dare-you-to-mention-the-game looks on their faces, which made Jake wonder why they'd bothered to come here in the first place.

Several unintuitive types shouted, "Great game," and the players shot them searing looks.

They headed to a table of girls, and Jake saw that next to that table sat a table of Goths, with Viper and Zeke among them, dressed entirely in black from their hair to their shoes. Zeke still had that camcorder to his eye, and as Grange approached the table next to him, Zeke got to his feet and zoomed in on the quarterback's face.

"Get that out of my face," Grange said through his teeth.

Zeke kept filming. "Again, but with more feeling."

Jake winced, knowing how this was going to turn out.

That was when Grange knocked the camcorder out of Zeke's hands. The Goths sprang to their feet and launched out at Grange, and Grange struck Zeke across the jaw, then suffered the attacks of Viper and another guy who looked like he'd been made up for a horror movie.

The next thing they knew, there was a pile of fighting bodies, and the girls in the booth were screaming like Hollywood starlets. The other students left their seats and surrounded them. Jake realized he was left at the booth alone, and he got slowly out and saw his friends yelling and trying to break up the fight. Andy was the school wrestling champion, and probably the only one qualified to pull rabid bodies away from one another. Slowly, but surely, they broke up the fight. Grange emerged with a bloodied lip and nose, and Zeke had a red spot on his jaw that would surely be a bruise the next day and an eye that looked as if it was swelling bigger every second. Friends held them back until Andy could untangle them all. By that time the manager intervened and ran all the fighters out to the parking lot, where the police were beginning to arrive.

Wearily, the guys came back to the table. Logan dropped in next to Jake, and Andy sat across from them. "What was that punk thinking?" Andy asked. "Sticking that camera in his face."

"Did you see his eye? And Grange's lip was busted bad."

"Man, Grange was stupid to knock the camera out of his hand," Andy said. "You'd think he'd be too tired to fight after all that energy he used up fumbling the ball tonight."

"Listen to you guys," Jake said. "You're no better than they are. Calling them names, insulting them behind their backs . . ."

"You want to do it to their faces?" Logan asked.

"No, I'm just saying we shouldn't be so surprised when they act like they're lost, because that is what they are. That's not what *we* are, so why are we acting like them? Those people are hurting, on both sides of that fight. Man, if we were doing our jobs, there wouldn't be any fighting."

"Why don't you shut up, Sheffield?" Andy said.

Jake gaped at him. His friend had never spoken to him that way, except in jest. There was no joking now. He swallowed back his pride, then nodded. "Okay. Let me out of here."

"Come on, you guys," Logan said. "Where are you going, Jake?"

"Let me out," he said. "Now!"

Logan slid out of the booth and let Jake out.

"Come on, Jake, I didn't mean it," Andy said. "Just chill, okay? You're stressing us out."

But Jake didn't answer him. He just bolted out the door.

He saw the police car that had come to ensure domestic tranquillity, and he leaned against the building trying to get a breath. He hadn't meant to go ballistic in there, but he couldn't believe his best friend had told him to shut up. It was just incredible.

But he couldn't dwell on that now, he thought. *Lord, are there people out here who need me?*

As if in answer, he heard a voice.

"I'll show them. I'll show them all. They won't treat me like a nobody again."

He looked around the bush next to him and saw Zeke standing in the trees, smoking a cigarette. "Hey, man," Jake said quietly.

Zeke just shot him a look.

"Sorry about your camcorder. And your . . . eye."

"Don't worry about it," Zeke said. "It's payback time. I've got it covered."

Jake didn't know what he meant by that, so he latched onto the need he'd heard. "I know you want to show them," he said. "But you know, you don't have to do that, because you are somebody. You're important, Zeke. I know you feel like people take you for granted, like you don't exist or something, but that's just because they don't know you."

Zeke just looked at him. "Who are you?"

"Jake. Jake Sheffield."

"And you know me how?"

"I go to your school." They were having a conversation, he thought. This was good. "But there is somebody who really knows you, Zeke. God knows you, inside and out, and he cared enough to die for you. Can you imagine how much love there would have to be for somebody to die for you?"

"I'm God's enemy," the voice said. "I'll die for hate, but so will they."

"I know you think you're an enemy of God," Jake said. "And you understand dying for hate . . . but Christ died for us while we were still his enemies. He knows more about us than we know about ourselves, Zeke. He knows you and wants you so bad that he's put you in my path several times today, and I just know I'm supposed to tell you all this."

Zeke took a drag and exhaled slowly. "You're a jock too, aren't you?"

Jake shrugged. "Well, I'm not on any school teams. I mean, I like to think I'm athletic . . . I play summer baseball and shoot hoops with my friends and stuff, but . . . I don't have a letter jacket or anything like that."

Zeke seemed to consider the cloud of smoke he blew out. "So you say God told you to tell me this stuff?"

"Not in words, no. He just made me care enough to come out here. You're somebody to him, Zeke. Somebody important enough to die for."

Zeke dropped his cigarette and stubbed it out beneath the toe of his boot. "I'm important enough for a lot of people to die for," he said, then shooting one last look at Grange, he headed out to the car where his friends were talking to the cop.

Jake just stood there for a moment, not sure how to take that. Was Zeke saying that he understood the death of Christ? Or was he implying something else?

He watched the four Goths get into the old station wagon with blackened windows, that looked very much like a hearse. The car limped away with its engine blowing and spitting. Jake looked across the parking lot and saw Lee Grange talking to another cop. Grange's friends were each at their own cars, and some of them left in the other direction. A couple were talking to girls at their cars, so Grange was alone with the cop.

Jake crossed the parking lot, and as the cop finished with him and Lee got into his car, Jake reached him. "Hey, Grange. How's that nose?"

It didn't look so good, but the big football player put on a good face. "No big deal." He took off his jacket and flung it in the window of his car. "What do you want? If you came to chide me about the game, I'll give you the same thing I gave him."

Jake held his hands up. "Don't worry. I didn't even see the game."

"You didn't miss anything." He leaned back against the fender and looked at his feet. "I don't know what was wrong with me tonight. I just couldn't seem to . . ." His voice trailed off, and he breathed a despairing sigh.

"I'll have to face the music. He'll grind my nose in it. Remind me what a loser I am."

The voice reminded Jake of what he'd heard that morning. It seemed so long ago. "Grange, do you have any idea at all what a winner you are?"

Grange looked up at him, suspicious. "Watch it, Sheffield. I'm not in a good mood."

"I'm serious," Jake said. "Grange, this morning when I was sitting across from you in the library, I felt this overwhelming sensation that God wanted me to care about you. That he wanted me to talk to you about him and tell you that you're not a loser, no matter what your father or your coach makes you think."

At that Grange straightened. Jake had his full attention.

"Grange, you're so much a winner . . . that I risked getting punched in the face to come talk to you. All you have to do is believe it. You don't need to get your feeling about yourself from what your father thinks of you. You just need God's approval. And that's not hard to get at all." Jake looked around and saw that Grange's friends were scattered and busy with others in the parking lot. "Look at this. God even orchestrated it so I could talk to you one on one. He's been waiting for you, Grange. Have you ever heard the story of the Prodigal Son?"

Grange shrugged. "I'm not sure."

"Well, the son of this rich dude asked for his inheritance so he could go live really high while he was young. So his dad gave it to him. But he was dumb and spent it all and wound up dirt broke with nothing to eat. He finally came back home, and it says that his father saw him while he was still a long way off. And he ran to his son and kissed him, and dressed him in royal clothes, and put a ring on his finger welcoming him back into the family, and threw this great big bash. Man, you're the son, and your Father—the one who sees you as a winner and not a loser—is watching the horizon for you to come back. He wants you so much that he prodded me to come out here and tell you. All you have to do is believe it. Instead of clenching those fists in anger, you can open your hands and reach up to God. He wants you, man."

Grange's eyes were locked on him as he went on, and Jake knew that, before the night was over, there would be one more celebration in heaven.

twelve

That night, Jake's mother was waiting up when he got home. She looked tired. She was in her robe and had taken her make-up off, and she looked older than she was as she busied herself cleaning the kitchen. "Hey, Mom," he said, dropping his keys on the table.

She kissed him on the cheek. "I've been worried about you today," she said. "I haven't seen you. You okay?"

"Yeah, I'm feeling a lot better," he said. "Mom, what happened to me today was a good thing. I mean, I did feel bad, but it turned out good."

"Good." She pulled a chair out from under the table and sat down. "Tell me about it."

He could see that she was weary, and he felt bad for her. She worked too many hours, and Jake's and Heather's part-time jobs didn't begin to supplement. He plopped into the chair across from her.

"I'm all alone. I have no one to depend on."

The words startled him, and he looked at his mother and realized he had just heard her soul. It confused him, because up until now, most of the Christians he'd heard had said things about bearing more fruit. The ones that talked of being alone and despairing usually weren't the ones who knew Christ. Yet his mother knew Jesus, didn't she?

The door opened and Heather burst in. "Hey, Mom. Oh, Jake, you're not gonna believe this. I talked to Trina Bradshaw after the game like you said, and you hit the nail right on the head. She was hurting, and, Jake, you're not gonna believe this but I led her to Christ. She's gonna come to church with me next Sunday. She wants to join the youth group and get into a Bible study. She's real excited about it."

Jake grinned. "Good going, Heather. Did you mention me?"

She grunted. "Give me a break. You said yourself—"

"You did that?" Alice cut in, gaping up at both of them.

"Sure, Mom. Jake and I have been leading people to Christ left and right today."

Jake gave his mother a shrug. "She might be exaggerating that a little."

"Well, maybe for myself," Heather said. "I only led a couple of people, but Jake . . . how many are you up to now?"

He shook his head. "I don't know. It doesn't matter."

"Sure, it matters." She pulled up a chair and sat down. "Who'd you talk to after the game?"'

The smile crept back to his face. "Grange."

"You talked to Lee Grange? Did he accept Christ?"

"He sure did. He's going to be there Sunday too."

She slapped her hand on the table. "Man! Mom, is this not the greatest thing you've ever heard?"

Alice looked a little stunned. "It is. I'm proud of you guys. Jake, what's come over you?"

Jake looked into his mom's eyes and wondered if he had been walking around in a daze, missing the fact that his mother was depressed and despairing. He decided that telling her about the voices he was hearing would only add to her depression. She would insist that he was sick and send him for counseling and a million other things that they couldn't afford. Then she'd probably melt and go back to the boyfriend who had recently dumped her.

"I don't know what happened," Jake said. "I just felt like God touched me today and said, 'Get out there and talk to these people. They're dying.'"

She got tears in her eyes and reached across the table to squeeze Jake's hand. "I used to feel that way myself," she said. "Back when I was a teenager and I first knew the Lord, I used to tell everybody I saw. I couldn't understand why everyone wasn't doing it."

Jake hung on to that, hoping it meant that she really did know the Lord. "What happened, Mom?"

"It faded," she said. She looked down at the table and swallowed. "You know that parable Jesus told about the four seeds?"

"Yeah."

"I may be the third one."

"Which one was that?" he asked, ashamed that he didn't know.

"I know!" Heather said.

They both looked at Heather. He might have known his sister would know.

"The one where the seed is planted and the thorns grow up and smother out the plant?" Heather asked her.

His mother nodded. "And Jesus said it represented the worries of the world and the deceitfulness of wealth, choking out the word. It becomes unfruitful. That's what I am."

Heather looked at her mom, her eyes suddenly stricken. "But, Mom," she said, "that verse is about unsaved people, isn't it? I mean, I've always thought the fourth seed was the only one that was a real Christian."

"I don't know," Alice said. "I guess deep down in my heart I'm still a believer. I still love Jesus. I've just lost that connection somehow."

"Mom, what's wrong?" Jake asked.

She dabbed at her eyes. "I'm just tired, Jake. Things at work have been really tough lately, and my breakup with James . . . It was the right thing, but it doesn't feel so good to be rejected. Then today I was worried about you."

"Mom, I'm so sorry I made you worry."

"It's okay. I worry about you kids if you're out at night, if you'll get home safely. I worry about things that are happening in the schools."

"Mom, the Bible tells us not to worry," Heather said. "It doesn't do any good."

Jake was surprised; he didn't know the Bible said that. He would have to look it up. He took his mother's hand and laced his fingers through hers. "You're not alone, Mom."

His mother's eyes met his.

"Mom, Jesus is with you. He's right there with you. He knows your every worry. He knows every thought in your head. He knows what your emotions are doing. He even knows what your soul needs, sometimes when *you* don't even know. He's with you, Mom."

"I know that intellectually," she said. She tapped her chest with her finger. "I've just got to remember it in here. Maybe I need to do what you're doing. Get out there and tell somebody about Jesus. Revive the fire that used to be inside of me."

Heather and Jake looked at each other and grinned. "Mom, you just would not believe how cool it is," Heather said.

Jake agreed. "It is, Mom. It's awesome. Lives were saved today."

"Eternities were saved," Heather added.

His mother sat back in her chair, and the years seemed to drain from her face. "So, what you're telling me is that after all my worrying, God was taking care of you guys, teaching you, growing you? That I'm not the one who has to teach you every spiritual lesson?"

"That's what we're telling you, Mom," Jake said. "He's a good teacher. Man, can he teach."

She leaned up on the table and propped her chin on her hand. "Tell me about what you did today with those people. Every little thing. Maybe your fire will be contagious."

thirteen

The next day was Saturday, and Jake woke up early, before anyone else in the house. The moment he got out of bed, he looked up to the ceiling and whispered, "What are you going to do with me today, Lord?"

A stirring in his soul sent him looking for his Bible, which he found in the backseat of the car he shared with Heather. He couldn't remember the last time he'd read it on his own without Gary telling him to turn to a certain passage.

He brought it into the house and opened it on the table. Photographs and notes fell out, along with candy and gum wrappers. He dropped his head on the table and began to pray and ask forgiveness. He asked the Lord to give him a crash course on his Word, so he would be able to speak accurately about the Bible if anyone asked. There was something wrong with him telling so many people about Jesus, when he knew so little himself. He took the Bible and got comfortable on the couch, turned on the lamp, and began to read. And as he did, his spirit was fed.

Hours later, when Heather and his mother had gotten up, Jake found that he had an itching in his soul to get back out into the world and tell more people about Jesus. Zeke's face kept coming to his mind, along with the conversation they'd had outside the Pizza Hut the night before. Zeke had tried to look uninterested, smoking his cigarette, and making biting comments about revenge, but Jake knew he had considered Jake's words. He knew the Lord was especially concerned about Zeke, and so he had made him cross Jake's path several times yesterday. He thought about how to go about getting in touch with the Goth, and realized that, since school wasn't in session today, his only choice was to go to Zeke's house. He didn't have a clue what Zeke's last name was, or where he lived, but he figured one of his friends must know.

It took three phone calls to get Zeke's last name. It was Kadzyk, and he learned that his first name was really Mike, but he'd gone by Zeke ever since anyone could remember. Jake scanned the phone book and found the name Kadzyk listed. There was only one in town. It had the address beside it, and Jake recognized the street.

He went into the living room where his mother and sister were watching the news on television.

"Heather, I need to take the car somewhere."

"Take off," she said. "I'm not going anywhere for a while."

"Mom, I'll be back later, okay?"

She looked up at him with sleepy eyes. "Where are you going?"

"To talk to a friend."

"What friend?"

Heather was getting interested, as if she knew he was going out to witness again.

"A guy named Mike Kadzyk. He goes by Zeke."

Heather's eyes opened wide in alarm. "You're going to talk to Zeke?"

"Yeah, why?"

"Because he's not gonna listen."

Jake shrugged. "I know, but for some reason, I think God's really put him on my heart today."

Heather only stared at him for a moment. "I'll pray for you, Jake."

His mother squeezed his hand. "Keep in touch, okay? Don't just disappear for the whole day."

He promised, then headed out the door.

Jake drove past Zeke's house three times before he figured out which one it was. He had expected it to be a rundown place that looked like something out of a dark movie with thunderstorms and fog, but instead, it was a nice, clean, middle-class home in a nice neighborhood. He wondered what Zeke's parents thought of his love for the color black, and his friend with the snake on his face, and the goatee and body piercing and black eyeliner, and all the things he represented, whatever they were. He wondered if his mom dressed like that too. Maybe they were a whole family of Goths, from his father on down to a baby clad in black Pampers.

The thought brought a grin to his face as he went to the door. He knocked on it, feeling nervous, and he said a quiet prayer for help from the Lord. A woman answered the door, jogging in place as loud music reverberated throughout the house. In the background, he could hear that little curly-haired aerobics guy counting on the television.

"Yes?" she asked, breathless. She had blond hair and wore a blue shirt with gym shorts. She looked so normal, she could have just emerged from playing Bunko with Jake's mom. It confused him.

"Uh . . . is this the Kadzyk house?"

"Yes. Can I help you?" she yelled over the noise and kept running in place.

"I'm . . . uh . . . here to see Zeke. Is he here by any chance?"

She looked a little surprised to see someone in color standing at her door. "Yeah, he's out working in the garage. You can go in through that door right there." She jogged out and pointed to the closed garage.

"Thanks," he said. The door closed behind him, and he followed the sidewalk to the garage. He could hear metal banging inside there, and he wondered what Zeke was doing. He knocked, then opened it and started to step inside. Zeke looked up from what he was doing. As if surprised, he quickly crossed the garage and pushed Jake back out. He closed the door behind him.

"What do you want?" Zeke snapped. His eye was black and almost swollen shut from the fight with Grange.

Jake thought he smelled gunpowder, but then he realized it was probably just the cigarette smoke on Zeke's clothes. Zeke was holding one as they spoke, and he didn't try to keep from blowing it into Jake's face.

"I know this is gonna sound weird," Jake said. "But I woke up this morning and felt this overwhelming sense that God wanted me to come talk to you again. He's not gonna give up, Zeke. He wants you bad."

Zeke blew out a laugh, dropped his cigarette onto the concrete, and stubbed it out with his toe. He picked it up and put it in his pocket. Jake imagined his mother throwing a fit over the cigarette stubs he and his friends left out in the yard. There had probably been some ultimatums given.

"I'm a nonentity. I don't even exist."

The voice came as a surprise to Jake. He didn't know why he hadn't expected it. "Don't you have any friends?" Zeke asked. "Why do you keep bugging me?"

"Zeke, you're not a nonentity."

Zeke's eyes shot to his. "What did you say?"

"I said you're not a nonentity. You do exist, and God knows it, and he can see right into your heart."

"Then he must be getting his eyes full," Zeke said.

"Zeke, Jesus cares enough about you to send me over here on a Saturday when I didn't even know your last name or where you lived. And, by the way, that's not because you're a nonentity; it's because you're in a different grade and I haven't known you."

"What do you want from me, man?" Zeke asked.

"I don't want anything from you," Jake said. "Nothing at all. I just want to tell you what God wants you to know."

"Oh, like you're really his spokesman. Did somebody tell you something about me?"

"No. I haven't talked to anybody who knows you. All I'm telling you is that God sent me."

"He sent you," Zeke repeated. "So, what did he do? Wake you up this morning and say, 'Go over to 233 Sycamore Drive and talk to Zeke'? Did he tell you I might be up to no good in my garage?"

Jake didn't know what Zeke was talking about. "No, nothing like that. He just wanted me to tell you about his love. You don't have to feel invisible and left out. You don't have to sink into darkness, and you don't have to keep on with this stuff you do. Picking fights with quarterbacks and videotaping everything . . ."

"Man, you don't know anything. Why don't you just get out of here?"

Jake realized he wasn't getting anywhere. "All right, I'm not gonna bother you anymore. I just want you to understand. I came and I told you what I was supposed to tell you. The rest is up to you. And look, we'd love to have you tomorrow at our church. You'd like our pastor, and you could even try Sunday school. I'd meet you out front if you wanted me to."

"Oh, yeah, that'd be fun," Zeke said sarcastically. "You can count on me. I'll sure be there. Gee, can we sing hymns and pass the plates?"

Jake got that feeling he'd had at the mall yesterday, when those seniors had laughed at him. "I really wish you'd come," he said. "It's at Mount Calvary, over on Bishop Drive. You know where it is."

Zeke chuckled. "Yeah, man. I know where it is."

Jake started to walk back down the driveway. But before he had made it too far, he turned back. "I know when I leave here, you're gonna think about what I said. God's working on you whether you like it or not. And I'm telling you, man, if you ever become a believer, your life is gonna change, and you're gonna know peace like you've never known before. You'll have joy. Who knows, you might crack a smile every now and then."

Zeke opened the door to the garage and stepped back inside. "I've gotta get back to work," he said.

"Well, I'll see you later. Maybe tomorrow?"

As Zeke closed the door behind him, his laughter echoed over the garage.

fourteen

Jake's mother was at the grocery store when he got back home, and Heather was doing aerobics to a tape on the television. She stopped jumping and kicking when Jake came in. "What happened?" she asked. "Did he accept Christ?"

He turned the television down. "What is it with you people and aerobics?"

She frowned. "What people?"

"Never mind. No, he didn't accept Christ. You were right. I don't know what made me think he would listen."

"God made you think he would listen," she said. "You know, you're not responsible for everybody you witness to. God's gonna draw them to him. All you have to do is be obedient."

He bounced down onto the couch. "Zeke worries me. A lot."

"Why?"

"I don't know. I just get this funny feeling. He's filled up with hate. I get the feeling he's out for revenge."

"Revenge against who?"

"I don't know. Grange, maybe. Some of the other football players. They got in a fight at Pizza Hut last night and came up with a couple bloody noses and some black eyes. I'm not sure Zeke is receptive to anything I've said."

"I don't think you should sweat it," Heather said. "You did what you were supposed to do, and God will do the rest. But don't concentrate on the one you lost. Concentrate on all those you won. And then go out there and do some more. I'm gonna do it today."

"You are?"

"Sure I am. I started thinking of all my friends who don't know the Lord, and I know them well enough to figure out what they need, you know, kind of like you, only I'm not hearing it in words. I'm just using what I know about them and trying to apply it to their spiritual condition. Does that make sense?"

"A lot of sense," Jake said.

"I thought of two people I really need to talk to, and I'm gonna meet them for lunch."

"Great," he said.

"Just hang in there, Jake. God'll give you some victories today, and he might give Zeke one before it's all over. By the way, can I borrow some money?"

"I don't have any."

"Yes, you do. I dug five dollars out of your bank."

"Heather!"

"Well, can I borrow it or not?"

"I guess so, but you have to pay me back."

"Yes!" she shouted. "Talk about victories."

"See, that's the thing," Jake said, going back to their original conversation. "I'm not sure Zeke's victory will be our victory."

"All we can do is pray," she said. "He may be a real tough guy, but he can't stand up to the power of prayer and the Holy Spirit working on him. You ought to know that by now."

fifteen

Jake had to work bagging groceries that afternoon at the grocery store a couple of blocks from his home. He heard the needs of every customer who came through the line, and he made a special effort to take their bags to their cars, even though some of them said they could do it themselves. It was unusual for him. Usually he did anything he could to get out of more work. But today he felt a special need to talk to the people whose souls were crying out.

At his best count, he figured he'd led at least six people to the Lord that day, and he'd invited somewhere between ten and fifteen to church, though he wasn't sure he'd counted right. By the time he got home, he realized that he didn't have anything planned for that night. That was the time when he and his buddies started calling each other to make plans to get together.

But when he got home, there were no calls from his friends. He started to feel bad about what had happened last night and wondered if Andy and Logan were still angry at him. He shouldn't have stormed out, he thought. He should have tried harder to understand their feelings, especially since they were the feelings he'd had just twenty-four hours earlier. He tried to call each of them, but they weren't home. Andy had a beeper, so he paged him and waited a while for him to call back. He never did.

Heather came to his door and looked in. "Did you borrow my CD player?"

"Yeah, the other day."

"I want it back," she said. "I need it."

He looked around his room and found it under a pile of dirty clothes. "Here," he said, thrusting it at her. He noticed that she was in full make-up and dressed to go out. "Where are you going?"

"Sophomore party," she said. "What are you gonna do tonight?"

He shrugged. "I don't know. I've made everybody mad. Nobody'll call me back."

"If your friends got mad at you for talking to them about witnessing, I would question whether they're even Christians or not."

"They are," he said. "I could hear their souls. They're Christians, just lazy ones, like I used to be."

The phone rang, and Jake dove for it, hoping it was Andy or Logan. Instead, it was a girl's voice. "Jake? Jake Sheffield?"

"Yes," he said.

"This is Beth Ann Lloyd. Remember, you talked to me yesterday at the food court?"

"Yes," he said. "Hi, how are you?"

"I'm fine. Really good." There was a thick pause, and finally she got the words out. "I've decided to have my baby."

He sat back on the bed and grinned up at Heather. "That's great."

"Yeah, I don't know yet if I'm gonna give it up for adoption or raise it myself."

"At least you have nine months to decide."

"Yeah, that's what I was thinking." She drew in a deep breath, as if she wanted to say something else. Then, finally, she went on, "Jake, I was wondering if I could ask you a favor. If you don't want to do it, just say so, okay?"

He braced himself, wondering what in the world a pregnant girl would want from him. "Well, sure. What?"

"I was wondering if you would come talk to my boyfriend tonight. He finally called and agreed to have dinner with me so we could talk. I'd really like it if you could kind of tell him some of the stuff you told me yesterday, about Jesus and everything."

Jake's eyebrows shot up. "Yes, I'd be glad to!"

"See, the reason he stood me up yesterday is that he's pretty confused, and I think he's depressed. He didn't want this anymore than I did. I think he might need to know what I found out. You know, about Jesus?"

"Of course, he does."

"And I hate to keep imposing, but if you don't mind, I'd really like you to talk to my sister too. She's a couple of years younger than me, and she's starting down the wrong path. I can see it already. And I'm not a very good example, because she knows the kind of stuff I've been doing."

Jake's heart leaped in his chest. "I'll talk to anybody you want me to talk to, Beth Ann. In fact, I'm yours tonight. You tell me where to go and who to talk to, and I'm there."

"All right," she said. "Meet me at the food court at seven o'clock."

Jake hung up the phone and turned back to Heather, a grin on his face.

"Who was that?" she asked.

"It was one of the girls I talked to yesterday. She wants me to come share the same thing with her boyfriend and her sister. Can you believe that?"

Heather slapped her thighs and held her palms out. "There you go. Your fruit is bearing fruit."

"My what?"

"Well, you've been so worried about your friends not wanting to get out there and help you witness, but God's taken care of it. Don't you see? The people you've led to Christ are leading other people to Christ. Look how it could multiply if all of us got out there and did it!"

"That's what I've been trying to tell them."

"Well, you don't need to tell them, you need to show them, and they're gonna see it before long. Jake, this is what Christianity is all about, isn't it?"

"Sure is."

"Then, let's get out there and quit focusing on the things that aren't working out. There's too much that is."

sixteen

That morning, Jake's mother got into a conversation with their neighbor across the street when she went out to get the paper and wound up leading the man to Christ. She came back in, dancing and singing, laughing like a teenager. Jake didn't think he had ever seen her so excited.

He was fifteen minutes late for Sunday school, and when he got to the door, he thought for a moment that he was at the wrong class. There seemed to be standing room only in the youth room. They were bringing in extra chairs. People were standing against the walls.

Jake stepped in and looked around. Beth Ann, the pregnant girl, was there with her boyfriend and her sister, both of whom Jake had led to Christ last night after he'd heard the boy's soul cry out that he had no future and the sister saying that she felt like a pig covered in slop. He had zeroed in on those thoughts and fears, and they had hung onto every word he'd said.

His eyes scanned the crowd, and he saw the blue-streaked girl to whom Heather had witnessed at the ball game. On the front row, Grange sat with some of his friends. Jake grinned, wondering what the kids from his school had thought when Franklin High's quarterback had shown up today.

Someone tapped on his shoulder, and he turned around and saw the black guy who worked at the arcade grinning down at him. "Hey, man, how's it going?"

"L. J.!" Jake laughed and shook his hand. "I didn't expect you to be here!"

"Hey, I never walk away from a challenge," he said. He had a new, shiny nose ring in for the occasion, and he wore the same worn-out blue jeans and tee shirt that he'd had on the other night.

Heather stepped into the room behind Jake. "Whoa!" she said, startled. "Look at this! Oh, my gosh, there's Trina!"

Jake followed her eyes and saw Trina sitting with some of Heather's friends, as if she'd been coming there all along. Andy and Logan sat together, looking around, unusually quiet at the new flurry of activity. Jake wondered what they were thinking.

Gary was at his best today. It was almost as if he had expected this and had planned for it. He spent the Sunday school hour talking about the lost sheep and how the shepherd left the ninety-nine to find it. And the lost coin and the lost son. It was the same message he'd given in youth group just a few days ago, but this time people listened. Jake, too, found himself riveted on his pastor, soaking in every word, writing down the Scripture references so he could find them later, hoping he could remember all of it by the time he left there.

After Sunday school, the youth group headed for the church service, and Jake tried to mix with all of those he had influenced into coming, but it was hard to get to them all. He stepped into the sanctuary and saw that it was full. They had even opened the balcony today, something that rarely happened. He wondered where all these people had come from. Then he sat down and looked around and saw different people he had helped yesterday at the grocery store. Some of them had brought spouses and children. Some had brought friends. Tears burst into his eyes, and he tried to blink them back. He couldn't start crying here, in front of everybody, like a blubbering idiot. But he couldn't hold it back.

And as the praise music started, he began to realize what true worship was. He had seen God work through him in totally unexpected ways. He was one of those clay jars, hardly worth anything, yet Jesus had used him for the most beautiful purpose. Jake didn't deserve it, and he didn't know what he had done to be chosen this way, but he felt overwhelmingly thankful as he praised the Lord.

He was still floating high when the service was over and the people began to file out.

He noticed one of the elders, Mr. Jordan, coming up the aisle against the traffic, his eyes set on Jake. Jake waited for the older man to reach him. He looked angry and wore his glasses low on the tip of his nose. His bald head shone with a slight sheen of perspiration.

"Young man, may I have a word with you?"

"Yes, sir, Mr. Jordan."

"Jake, they tell me that you were the one responsible for this crowd that came here today."

Jake tried to look humble. "Well, not me, really. I mean, I talked to some of them, but the Holy Spirit is the one who got them here."

"I beg to differ with you," Mr. Jordan said. "I don't believe the Holy Spirit would have brought people like that into our church."

Jake stared at him. "What do you mean, 'people like that'?"

"I mean, people with blue streaks in their hair. Kids with nose rings, tattoos, goatees. People of other races. Women coming into the Lord's house with black roots and dirty hair, dressing in things that are completely inappropriate. This is a holy place, you know. We don't need to defile it with behavior such as this. Not to mention the air conditioning."

Jake squinted as he tried to make the connection. "Air conditioning?"

"Yes. With all these extra people it's just too hot in here, and I don't suppose you've thought about how we'll pay the electric bill. These people don't look like big tithers to me. They won't be able to carry their own weight."

"Uh, yes, sir." Jake felt as if he was in over his head. He'd never run up against an elder before. Usually, they ignored the youth. "I understand your point, but some of these people are brand-new Christians. They might not exactly know how they're supposed to look when they come to church, but we need to be patient with them. I'm just so glad they came."

"You're not listening! They are not welcome here," the elder hissed. "I'm suspicious of their being here in the first place. I don't know what they're up to or what they're trying to prove. I expect you to do something about it."

Jake's mouth fell open, and the church seemed to get hotter. "Do what about it? What in the world is there to do? I thought we were all about seeking the lost. Isn't that what Jesus did?"

"If the lost were truly repentant, they wouldn't come into this house looking like that."

Jake's mouth began to tremble. "You know, I'm not much of a Bible scholar. You probably know a whole lot more Scripture than I do. But I have read the Gospels, and I don't remember one single time when Jesus told someone they didn't dress right for him, that they weren't acceptable. If he didn't do it, I don't think we ought to do it, either."

He saw Gary coming up the aisle, grinning from ear to ear, almost bouncing in his shoes. Jake hated for his joy to be spoiled, but there was no way around it.

Then he heard the voice coming from Mr. Jordan. "They have to see who's in charge. It's slipping away. I can't let it slip away."

Jake let the voice sink in, and he hung on the words for a moment, turning them over in his mind and measuring them against what Mr. Jordan was saying out loud. And then he knew. This man, who made so many of the decisions in their church, didn't know Christ at all. What he had was a head knowledge, but it didn't give him as much understanding of Jesus as those who had come today with nose rings and tattoos and streaks in their hair. Jake suddenly felt a compassion for the man and wanted to reach out and tell him that he didn't have to worry about losing his place or being in control, because there was someone better in control, and Jesus wouldn't botch up the job. But Jake feared he would never accept that.

When the elder expressed his concern to Gary, the youth pastor's jubilation faded. The senior pastor joined them to see what the problem was. The moment the elder voiced his concerns, Brother Harold nipped it in the bud.

"Al, I've got news for you," he said. "This church is a place for lost souls. As the body of Christ, we are about bringing people here who don't know him. And when they come, I'm not gonna criticize what they're wearing or how they look, I'm just gonna thank and praise God for trusting us with them. If you have a problem with it, take it to God, and let him explain it to you."

Al Jordan's ears turned red. "You've made your choice, pastor." And with a look on his face that threatened something, though none of them knew quite what, he turned and bolted out of the sanctuary. Gary breathed a deep sigh and looked at the pastor. "Do you think he'll leave the church?"

"Possibly," Brother Harold said. "But that's okay." He set his hand on Jake's shoulder. "Jake, you just keep on doing what you've been doing, and I commit to do my best to get you as many helpers as I can."

"Thanks," he said. "Sorry about making him mad. I never dreamed anybody would get offended by visitors."

When Brother Harold had been pulled away to introduce himself to more people, Jake took Gary aside. "Gary, Mr. Jordan's not a Christian," he whispered. "I heard his voice. He was worried about losing control. It's real important to him. He likes to be in charge. I got the distinct impression that he doesn't know Christ."

Gary closed his eyes. "No wonder. That explains a lot."

"So what are we gonna do?" Jake asked. "I mean, we can't just let him walk, can we? We have to tell him."

"Jake, remember what I told you the other day about people knowing just enough religion to be inoculated? Sort of a Christianity vaccine?"

"Yeah."

"Well, that may be what Al Jordan has."

"You thought that about Lou too. But God proved you wrong."

Gary looked at him for a moment, studying his face, then finally he began to smile. "You're right. He did."

"So what do we do? Just wave good-bye?"

"No," Gary said. "I promise, Brother Harold and I will go visit him today. Pray for us, okay? And pray for him."

"I will."

When Gary had moved on, Jake looked around for Andy and Logan. They had already gone. He wondered what they thought about all these people coming today. Were they rejoicing, like he was? Or were they still angry?

If they were, he'd just have to accept it. Jesus had promised there would be trials and tribulations. Some people would even hate him. He hoped that his friends weren't like the elder, disgusted by the people who had come to bring their sins to the cross . . . disgusted by the person who had brought them.

Instead of going home that afternoon, Jake's mother decided to celebrate by taking them out to eat. She was still excited and glowing with the joy of the Lord. Her eyes glistened as she talked about how proud she was of her children, and how her life had been rejuvenated in the last few days, how she finally felt she had a purpose, and that she wasn't alone. She talked on and on about how depressed she had been after her breakup. But now God had shown her, through Jake and Heather, that he was a husband to her, that he was helping raise her children, that she was anything but alone.

Later that afternoon, Jake and Heather went back to church for Gary's evangelism class. Jake had hopes that the classroom would be as full as it had been that morning, that all of the Christians of their youth group would want to learn to share their faith with as many others as they could.

When he got there, he saw that Gary was still excited, though the class wasn't nearly full. "This is all that came?" Jake asked.

Gary nodded. "I'd say there are fifteen here, but that's good, Jake. Last week there were only two or three. And they were the staff members' kids. I don't even think they had a choice in coming."

"But . . . this morning. So many people came up to me and congratulated me for bringing so many . . . You'd think they'd want to learn how to do it too."

"Well, maybe they're doing it on their own."

But somehow, Jake didn't think that was true. They were probably taking their Sunday afternoon naps, watching football, shopping at the mall.

Jake took his seat next to Heather as Gary went to the front and led the group in prayer, then began to outline what he hoped to do in the class. Jake heard a rustling at the door and turned around and saw Andy shuffling in. Their eyes met, and Andy lifted his eyebrows in kind of a halfhearted shrug and came to sit down beside him. Jake grinned and held out a hand for Andy to shake.

The smile that Andy shot him, and the pat on his knee, told Jake all was forgiven.

After a few moments, Logan came in, took a seat behind him, and leaned up to pat Jake on the shoulder.

Gary gave them some key Bible verses and a brief outline of the gospel so their minds wouldn't draw a blank when they reached that moment of truth. Several of the members expressed fears at what they were committing to do, but they all made the decision that they were going to live evangelistic lives from then on.

After the class, Jake and his buddies hung around in the room. "Sorry about Friday night," Andy said. "You were right. You just hit a nerve, that's all. I don't really like having my shortcomings thrown in my face like that."

"I didn't mean to throw them in your face," Jake said. "I just wanted you to see what it's like."

Logan nodded. "We saw what it was like this morning, Jake, with all those people here. It's hard to believe that through one person so many people would come, but . . ."

"We've been hearing about all the stuff you've been doing," Andy said. "My mom was talking to a friend you witnessed to at the grocery store yesterday. She came home really impressed, and then my dad said some of the interns in his office had talked to you somewhere and that they had changed and were talking about what Jesus had done in their lives."

"We got to thinking," Logan said. "We've got to get out there and do what you're doing. If you can do it, we can. God equipped all of us, didn't he?"

"Of course!" Jake said. "We can do it now, man. We head out somewhere and just start telling people. You won't believe how hungry they are. Man, with you two walking beside me, we can reach three times as many people. Think what next Sunday'll look like if we do that. We can go right now."

"Wait a minute." Andy took a step back and raised a hand to stop him. "Man, I know this is gonna sound like another excuse, but I can't go tonight. I feel like I need to bone up a little on all the Scripture Gary gave us and study what I need to say and . . ."

"Man, you know what Jesus did for you. That's all you need to tell them. Remember when Jesus healed the blind man, and the Pharisees took him aside and asked him to tell them what had happened? That blind guy didn't know a lot of Scripture, didn't know much of anything about Jesus. He just told them, 'One thing I do know. I was blind but now I see!' That was his testimony, and it was good enough for Jesus."

"But I feel the same way Andy feels," Logan told him. "It's like I'm not ready to fly without a net, you know?"

"Then bring your net," Jake said. "Bring notes, for Pete's sake. You can do that." Andy and Logan just exchanged uncomfortable looks.

"Come on, you guys! You're just starting to see what you need to be doing. Why don't you get out there and do it? I need help, man! There are too many of them. The harvest is white. Do you know what that means? It's gray when it's ripe. The white harvest means it's almost too late. There's no time to wait."

"We will help you," Andy said. "We promise. But today we just wanted to let you know that we're with you and we're sorry we acted like jerks Friday night. We're gonna get this right. But meanwhile I was thinking. Since we've got all these new Christians coming to our church, maybe we need to do something really special for them, make them feel like a part of things. I was thinking that maybe Gary would let us throw a party Friday night. Get a live Christian band and a bunch of food and just celebrate the fact that there are new Christians in the group. We could invite all the ones who came, even the ones who aren't youth."

"We could make it churchwide," Logan said. "You think they'd go for it?"

Jake grinned. "I think it's a good idea."

Gary, who'd been talking to some of the students in the hall, came back in, and Jake looked up at him. "Gary, the guys have just come up with a great idea. What would you say to throwing a party to celebrate all the new people who've come to Christ?"

Gary's eyes lit up. "I'd say it's the perfect time to get them all baptized too. Let's go talk to the pastor right now. If they're celebrating in heaven, we can celebrate down here."

seventeen

By the time Friday night rolled around, the party plans had been made. Jake hadn't helped, for he'd been taking extra shifts at the grocery store at night so he could talk to more people. Heather and his mother had helped with some of the plans and were both excited about the way it was shaping up. As far as Jake knew, most of the people he had led to Christ had agreed to come.

When he got there, they treated him like the conquering hero. He wasn't comfortable with the role, since he knew they weren't aware of the tremendous gift he'd been given and why things had worked so well for him. Anyone could have done it. God had made it easy for him.

He sat through the baptisms, but afterword, as the band played and Gary got up at intervals to thank the Lord for the harvest and for these new people who were coming to them for discipleship, Jake started feeling that stirring in his soul again. He had to get out of here, he thought. There were people out there who still hadn't heard. People with needs that he could meet. If he slipped away, no one would notice he was gone.

"Hi, Jake." He turned and saw Trina Bradshaw, wearing a gold lamé blouse over a pair of black jeans. She swept her hair back from her face and let it fall haphazardly over itself.

He straightened. "Hi, Trina." He wondered why she had approached him. Had Heather told her that he had a crush on her? He'd kill his sister if she had, he thought.

"I want to make others feel like this."

He heard her voice and knew from the depths of his soul that Heather had done a good job of leading her all the way to Christ. "You know, you can make others feel the way you feel," he said. "Lots of other people."

She looked at him as if she knew, somehow, that he had eavesdropped on her soul. Those radiant blue eyes got a slight grin in them. "Will you teach me?" she asked. "I want to be bold, like you."

He laughed. "I'm not bold. I'm just driven." He dared to meet her eyes. They were even better looking close up than they had been from a distance. "Look, there's a concert at the coliseum tonight," he said. "That big heavy-metal group is coming in, and I was just thinking that maybe I could kind of hang around in the parking lot, and when the concert starts letting out, I could talk to some more people. You wanna come with me?"

A smile crept across her face. "Yeah. Right now?"

"I was thinking it would be good. I'm a little antsy sitting here with people who already know Christ, when so many out there don't."

Her eyes softened again. "That's the thing about you, Jake. You care. I think that's cool."

His heart pounded as he left her there for a moment and found Gary to tell him where he was going. Gary patted his back and told him that was fine.

"Just one other thing. Uh . . . Trina Bradshaw. She wants to go with me. Only . . . is that wrong? I mean, it doesn't seem like I should get the great gift and the blessings of all these people coming to Christ . . . and get the girl too. I mean, this isn't about my love life."

"Then don't make it about your love life. Keep your focus, and God will take care of the rest. Think of it this way. You never had Trina's attention before. Now, out of the blue, she comes up to you? God is a better matchmaker than we are, Jake."

"Then, you don't think he'd mind if I took her with me tonight? Taught her how to witness?"

"I don't think he'd mind at all."

Trina was obviously nervous as she got into the car with Jake. All the way to the coliseum, she fidgeted. "Are you nervous about talking to people?" he asked finally.

She looked over at him. "Kind of. And maybe . . . a little nervous with you."

"Me?" he asked, chuckling. "Why?"

"Because you're so . . . real. And I don't know what I am."

"You're real too."

She smiled. "I just mean . . . I know how to play the game. With guys, you know. But lately, all the rules seem to have changed. I see things differently."

"I know," he said.

"So it's kind of like starting over. Learning the ropes again. Figuring out what to say to a real guy in a car, when he's not trying to impress me, and I don't really have to impress him."

He glanced over at her and saw the light from oncoming headlights skirting across her face. Her words settled into his heart like rain soaking into thirsty ground. He had always thought he would have to impress Trina to get her attention; he just hadn't figured out how to do it yet. He didn't have trophies and athletic honors, didn't get voted "Best" Anything at school, wasn't considered one of the nicest looking, didn't even make exceptionally good grades.

But Trina seemed to like him. Talk about signs and wonders.

They reached the coliseum, and he rolled the windows down and stayed in the car, waiting for the concert to break up. He could hear the bass notes from the concert reverberating even this far out.

"I would be in there tonight if I hadn't gotten saved," Trina said. "I had tickets."

He smiled. "If that band had come a week ago, I probably would have gone too. There are probably a lot of Christians in there. They're all partying and dancing and totally oblivious to the hurting people around them. And the hurting people on the stage."

"Why is that?" Trina asked. "Why would anyone want to keep that to themselves? I mean, when I see a good movie, I tell everybody I know because I want them to see it too. Why wouldn't I want to tell them about Jesus?"

"It's just fear," Jake said. "We're afraid people will think we're kooks. We don't want them to label us fanatics or write us off as religious freaks."

"But who cares what they say? A man died. And he rose again. So really, what difference does it make if people laugh at us? We've got Jesus on our side, and one day, they're gonna find out that he is Lord for sure, one way or another."

Jake swallowed the lump forming in his throat. "You learn fast."

"Heather was a good teacher."

"No, the Holy Spirit is a good teacher. Heather can talk, but your heart had to be open to the Holy Spirit."

"My heart's been open a long time. Nobody told me before." She got tears in her eyes and blinked them back. "When I think of all the stuff I wouldn't have done if I had just known earlier. So many things could have been different."

Jake felt crushing remorse and reached across the seat to take her hand. "Trina, I'm sorry I didn't tell you. But the truth is, I've been more worried about how to get you to notice me, than how to get you to notice Christ. It never occurred to me, until a few days ago, that you might need to hear."

"It's okay," she said. "I'm here now. And maybe I won't slip into that passive Christianity, hoping someone else will go out there and share. That's why I wanted to come here with you tonight, Jake. I want to start from the very beginning, looking for people who are like me. People desperate to know, if only somebody would tell them. I want to be a heart reader, like you."

He grinned. "A heart reader? What makes you think I read hearts?"

"Because you read mine," she said. "The other night, when you said those things about my beauty inside . . . I don't know how you did it, but you did. I want to do it too."

Jake felt so inadequate next to her. Here she was, a baby Christian on fire for Christ. He'd been a Christian for years, and it took God zapping him to wake him up. He was humbled by her and humbled at the lengths God had gone to show him how Christianity was supposed to work. "Let's pray, Trina. The concert will be over soon."

They held hands and prayed as the muffled music kept playing. After a while, he heard footsteps approaching in the gravel, and he looked up as Andy and Logan reached his car.

"Man, we thought we'd never find you."

He laughed and got out. Trina got out on the other side, and both guys gave her a double take. "Hey, Trina."

"We didn't know you were together."

"Trina wanted to come help me," Jake said. "How did you guys know where I was?"

"Gary told us where you were coming, man. We decided it was time for us to help. But you're gonna have to be patient with us. We're not too good at this."

"You can do it, man. It'll be great. Do the best you can. Think about how much pain is on the inside of some of these people. Think of it as a cancer, and you've got a cure."

Even as he spoke, the doors to the coliseum opened and people started pouring out. "Are you guys ready?" he asked.

They all looked nervous. Jake looked at Trina, saw that her face glowed with anticipation.

"Just come with me for the first couple," he said. "Then when you feel like you can, branch out on your own."

By the time the parking lot had emptied, Jake had led eight more people to Christ. Andy had spent the whole time talking to one anorexic girl, and Logan and Trina had teamed up to talk to a couple who would have lost their virginity that night if they hadn't run into them.

The four of them shouted like madmen and fools all the way home, elated that the Lord had found a way to use them.

eighteen

Jake couldn't get to his bedroom fast enough that night. He had yearned to thank God properly all the way home, and now he dropped to his knees beside the bed and began to pray. The Lord's goodness ached through his heart, bringing tears to his eyes. He asked again why he had been chosen for this.

People had come to Christ, his friends had become more fruitful, the girl he liked had started her Christian life discipled by him. He was just some skinny kid with few skills and a lot of hang-ups, yet God had touched his ears and opened them. God had led him to look for the sheep, the coin, the son. He had allowed Jake to enter into the joy of his master.

The longer he prayed, the more deeply he wept, for the feelings long squelched within his spirit were emerging to the surface.

"I'm so unworthy," he cried. "I don't know why you gave me this gift, and I'm so sorry I called it a curse when I first got it. But thank you for giving me a glimpse into how tormented people are. Thank you for showing me their wounds and their memories. Thank you for letting me hear their pain and their doubts and their self-hatred. Please lead me to all of them, Lord. As many as I can reach. Take me to them, Lord, and I'll tell them about you. Here I am. Send me."

He got into bed and lay still for a moment, tears running down his face, and he basked in the love of Christ, warming and comforting him like a soft blanket. He was loved, he thought as he drifted to sleep. He was chosen. He was used.

Just on the edge of sleep, he saw a divine finger motioning him to come. And then he heard a sheep bleating, and he turned and saw one running off into the brush, only this time there wasn't a shepherd chasing it down. It was only him, clad in blue jeans and tennis shoes, no longer a spectator as he leaped over branches and twigs, went around bushes, desperately trying to catch the little lost sheep. And then he caught it and felt the joy that he'd been feeling for the past several days whenever he led someone to the flock. Praising God, he carried it back.

And then the dream changed, and there was only the voice. The same voice he'd heard in the first dream, several days ago. Only this time, the words were different.

"And lo, I will be with you always, even until the end of the age."

Jake sat up straight in bed, fully awake, and realized he was sweating like he had in the dream. He shuddered. God had spoken again. There was no question this time. He knew the voice. He got out of bed and stumbled to the bathroom, washed the sweat off his face, and looked up at himself in the mirror as the rivulets of water dripped from his chin.

What did it mean?

God had not spoken to him before without changing his life. Was he changing it again, or was it just a message to keep him on the right track?

He went back to bed and lay there staring at the ceiling, trying to sleep, but sleep wouldn't come. When dawn finally broke through his window, he got up. A sense of unease stirred through him, and he didn't know what to attribute it to. But something was different. *He* was different somehow.

It was Saturday, so he left the house and went to a fast-food restaurant famous for its breakfasts. He got his food and a Coke and sat at a table, sipping it and waiting. People milled around him, high heels clicking and tennis shoes squeaking. Children whined, and a mother passed him with a baby who needed a diaper change. He heard people talking, bells ringing, cash registers opening.

Then he realized it.

He wasn't hearing their souls.

Startled, he got up and went to stand behind a crowd of a dozen or so people in line. He looked around him, waiting. He heard nothing but the idle chatter that came from their mouths. Nothing significant, nothing relevant.

Nothing everyone else couldn't hear.

He stepped back, suddenly aware that there had been a reason for the dream. God had taken the gift back from him. He turned from his right to his left, panicked, without a clue what to do. Abandoning his food, he ran out into the parking lot. A van load of teenagers on a trip somewhere were filing out, and he let himself get mixed among them. He listened, listened with all his heart and soul and might, listened as he knew God listened.

But he didn't *hear*.

It was gone. The gift had vanished, and he felt abandoned, disrobed and disarmed. He got into his car and sped home, wanting to go in and hide under the covers and figure this out.

When he ran into his house, he saw his mother in the kitchen. "Morning, Jake. You're up early. Where've you been?"

"Hardee's. Where's Heather?" he asked.

"In her room."

He ran through the house and into his sister's room. She sat up in bed reading.

"Heather, it's gone."

She looked up at him. "What is?"

"The gift! God took it back."

She slid her legs over the side of the bed and sat up stiffly. "He couldn't have."

"I had another dream," he said. "God spoke to me again, and when I woke up, it was gone."

"Well, how do you know? It's just you and me here."

"I went to Hardee's. There were people there, buying breakfast, and I stood there with them—I didn't hear anything."

"Well, maybe there was nothing to hear. Maybe God just didn't want you to hear their particular souls."

"No, there were dozens of people there. I tried it. I stepped into this crowd getting out of a van. Nothing!"

Heather got out of bed, looking ridiculous in a pair of plaid boxer shorts and a big football tee shirt. Her hair was all messed up, and Jake would have been amused if he hadn't been so upset. "Why would he take it away from me?" he asked. "I mean, I know I'm not worthy, but I wasn't worthy before, and he gave it to me, so why now? Just when things were starting to go well. Last night, Trina and Andy and Logan all led people to Christ. They're all on fire, and they want to do it again. What am I gonna do? How am I gonna help them now?"

"Wow. I don't know." She squinted up at him. "Trina went with you? I wondered where she was."

"Yeah . . . she came with me and we had a good talk. We prayed together, and then we talked to people coming out of the concert. I thought maybe I could ask her out. Maybe take her to a movie . . . but now this. She won't like me if I'm like everybody else. *I* won't like me. God won't like me."

"Now, wait a minute," Heather said. "God did this. Of course he's not going to blame you for it."

"But I said so many horrible things about it being a curse. I didn't expect him to get mad days later when I finally thanked him for it. I just don't understand. It seems so cruel to give me a taste of what the Holy Spirit hears and then take it from me. To open my ears, then close them again."

"Well, I guess God is God," Heather said. "He can do whatever he wants to."

"But there are so many out there that I didn't reach. There are so many people that I still need to talk to. I wasn't finished. The harvest is still white."

She looked into the mirror and grabbed a brush, ran it through her hair. Pensively, she set it back down. "You can still do that, Jake. You can still go out there and tell people about Jesus. This isn't going to change the fire that you lit under me, or Andy, or Logan, or Mom . . . any of them. They didn't even know about the gift."

"But don't you see? They're depending on me to be their leader in the whole thing, and here I am, with the rug snatched out from under me."

She looked at him for a moment, trying to think the situation through. "Why don't you tell Mom?"

"What can she do? I never told her to begin with. She'll have me committed."

"I don't think so, Jake. I think she'll believe you after all that's happened."

"I can't do it," he said. "Maybe I need to talk to Gary."

"Yeah," she said. "Good idea. Go talk to him. He'll tell you that your witnessing days aren't over. That you can still lead people to Christ. I've been doing it, and I didn't have any special gift."

"It's not the same," he said. "You were able to do it because I got you started. I got you energized. I told you what Trina was thinking."

"But you didn't tell me about all of them," she said. "Some of them I witnessed to without you helping."

"Still. It's not the same, talking to someone when you can't hear their needs. Starting a conversation without having that edge."

"Go talk to Gary, Jake," she said. "I don't know what to do for you."

nineteen

Jake headed over to Gary's house, hoping he was up. He felt a little guilty for interrupting his family on a Saturday morning, but he figured Gary would forgive him. Gary needed to know about this, after all. So many plans were being made for the church. They all assumed that Jake would keep bringing the people in, that they would keep celebrating, and eventually have to start a building fund and build a whole new sanctuary to fit the multitudes. That would all come to a halt now.

He pulled into the driveway and saw Gary out in the front yard digging a hole in his garden. From the knees and elbows down, he was covered with dirt, and he looked up and grinned as Jake pulled in.

"Whatcha know, Jake?" he asked as Jake got out of the car. His smile faded as he saw the slump in Jake's shoulders and the expression on his face. "What's the matter, man?"

Jake tried not to look pitiful. "I lost the gift."

"You what?"

"It's gone."

"No way!" Gary said. "Jake, what happened?"

Jake shook his head helplessly. "Gary, I had another dream last night, and when I woke up, it was gone. I went to Hardee's, stood around crowds. I couldn't hear a thing."

Gary's face went slack. Jake realized he might be as disappointed as Jake, himself, was. "Man," he said. "I had a whole calendar full of stuff. We were gonna have more of those celebrations for the new Christians. And we've already called the rental place and gotten extra chairs for the sanctuary. We've even had people come forward to do Bible studies, just to disciple the new converts. Some of our church members have decided that they need to get closer to the Holy Spirit and start studying their Bibles so they could bear more fruit. It's all kind of centered around this gift of yours."

Jake sat slowly down on the edge of the porch, looking down at the dirt at his feet. "I'm sorry, man. I don't know what happened. I let everybody down. I let God down, so he took it back."

Gary abandoned his shovel and came to sit next to him. "Man, you didn't let anybody down. I'll bet God is as proud of you as he can be. I hate that I put that much pressure on you. I didn't mean to."

"You didn't put any pressure on me," Jake said. "You just taught me how to use the gift."

"I know, but I didn't count on it being taken away."

"Neither did I." Jake sighed and shook his head. "I guess I just go back to my own mediocre existence, leading a fruitless life."

"No way," Gary said. "Not you. Not anymore."

"Well, how can I do anything different, when I've had a taste of something that's been snatched away?"

"You were touched by God. Do you know what I would give to have a touch like that? But God didn't touch *me* that way, he touched you. And he didn't do it for some cruel purpose. He did it to give you a glimpse of what he hears. Don't you think he wanted to give you a passion for winning souls to Christ? Don't you think he wanted to develop the kind of compassion within you that he has?"

"I don't know," Jake said. The corners of his lips were twitching as he struggled to hold back those wimpy tears that lay in ambush. "I was getting used to it. I had so much confidence. I could just go up to strangers and start a conversation, without worrying how it was going to turn out, because God was giving me clues into them, and he was giving me the words."

"He can still do that," Gary said. "He's been doing that for me for years. I didn't have to hear exactly what he heard."

"But I'm not like you," Jake said. "I needed the gift. It was the power. It was what drew people to Christ."

"No, the Holy Spirit drew people to Christ. All you did was overhear."

"I need to *keep* overhearing," Jake said.

Gary sat there for a moment, trying to think. Jake felt kind of bad for bringing this on him. He knew they had never taught him about how to deal with this kind of thing in seminary. Gary was probably wishing Jake had never brought him into this in the first place.

After a moment, Gary patted Jake on the knee. "You know, man, what we really ought to do is pray. Not work on figuring this out for ourselves. We need to pray and ask God what he wants you to do next."

Jake wiped the tears creeping out of his eyes. "He said something again . . . in my dream. 'And lo, I am with you always, even unto the end of the age.'"

Gary laughed softly. "I love it. He's a good God."

Jake looked at him. "Why do you say that?"

"Because those are the last words he spoke in the Gospel of Matthew," he said. "He gave the disciples the Great Commission, and he ended it with that, just before he ascended to heaven."

"So why did he want that to be the last spiritual voice I heard?"

"Because he wanted you to know that, even though he's pulled the gift away from you, he hasn't taken the Holy Spirit back. He's with you, Jake. He hasn't left you. He'll be with you every time you open your mouth to tell someone about him. But look what we all learned, Jake. We learned what a difference *one person* can make. You brought revival to our youth group . . . to the whole church . . . maybe to the town. You started a fire, Jake. And now so many people at our church realize that they could start fires too. God used you to teach us that."

"Then how come I feel like I did something wrong and I'm being punished again?"

"Because you're thinking wrong. Let's go to the Lord and ask him to straighten your thinking out, okay?"

When they had finished praying, Gary walked Jake back to his car. He had forgotten about all the dirt on his knees and his hands. "Jake, I know you've been thrown for a loop. I know you're upset. But just act like nothing ever happened. Just go on telling people about Jesus. Don't give it up. You've come too far. And listen, I got e-mail from Andy and Logan last night, and they told me about all the people you guys led to Christ after the concert. They were so excited. They asked me if we could go out witnessing during class time tomorrow night. Can you believe it? I want you there, Jake. I need you to go out with us and help the new people get started."

Jake gave a cynical laugh. "I can't do it."

"Yes, you can," Gary told him. "I won't take no for an answer. You love it too much to stop now. You know too much, Jake. You have to come and help us."

"I'll think about it," Jake said. But as he drove away, he knew he'd already made up his mind.

twenty

The next morning, Jake pretended to be sick and stayed home from church while his sister and mother went. He lay in bed, nursing his wounds, telling himself that he couldn't stand the thought of being in a crowd where he didn't hear voices, of seeing the faces of people who attributed their salvation to things he had told them. He couldn't stand the thought of having a conversation with them and not knowing what their deepest needs were. They would see through him, he thought. They would see that he was a fraud. That something had changed, and he couldn't explain it. He could never explain it.

When his mother and sister finally got home, he was out of bed watching television, staring at the screen as a World War II movie played.

"Feeling better, Jake?" his mother asked.

He shrugged. "Yeah, I guess."

"Well, let me just warm up the casserole and we'll have lunch soon."

She disappeared into the kitchen, and Heather dropped down onto the couch next to him. "They brought in extra chairs," she said. "There was standing room only. Some of the kids from the concert last night came. The pastor told them that if they wanted to talk to someone after church, they could come to the fellowship hall. Twenty-five people came."

He kept his gaze on the television screen. "Good. That's real good."

She stared at him for a moment and finally got up and put herself between him and the set. He had no choice but to look at her.

"You're pathetic, you know that?" she asked.

"Heather, I'm just sitting here minding my own business."

"You're sitting here wimping out, pretending to be sick to keep from going to church. What is wrong with this picture? Do you think God is gonna honor your pout? That just because you were touched by him, that now you can throw that gift back in his face?"

"I didn't throw it back in his face. He took it from me."

"Well, maybe he thought you had enough backbone to go ahead without it. Just like Andy and Logan have done. They didn't have a gift last night, and you weren't feeding all of it to them, because they told me they were all over that parking lot, talking to different people, and you weren't with them the whole time."

"Okay, so they were able to lead a few people to Christ."

"How do you think the Christian church got where it is today?" she demanded, crossing her arms. For a little thing, she sure looked menacing standing there in front of him. "It got there because people who had the Holy Spirit told people and they told other people and they told other people, and for two thousand years it's gone that way, and it's still surviving today. And you know what, Jake? They did it all without being able to hear a thing in each other's souls."

"Get off my back, will you? I didn't do anything. I was given a gift that I didn't ask for, and it was taken away from me. It's totally out of my control."

"So now you can just sit on that couch and watch TV on Sunday mornings and become useless as a Christian, like you were before."

"I am not useless!"

She was starting to cry, like she always did when she was angry. "Jake, I was so proud of you this last week," she said. "I saw what you were doing, and I thought it was the coolest thing in the world. It's the first time in my whole life I've wanted to be like you. But now you make me sick!"

He sprang off of the couch. "Well, thanks a lot for your support. I appreciate that. Kick me while I'm down, why don't you?"

"I guess you're just too good to go out there and get your hands dirty like the rest of us. You have to be divinely enlightened first. You have to have inside information. Heaven forbid you should ever have to go out on a limb and start a conversation without knowing how it's gonna end up."

"Hey, I never knew how they were gonna end up."

"No, but you had a pretty good idea what those people needed." She grabbed the remote control out of his hand and clicked the television off. "Why don't you go get your Bible, Jake, and read it, and get down on your knees and start asking God what he wanted you to learn from that experience, instead of sitting here wallowing in your self-pity."

Jake's face was hot. "You don't even know what you're talking about, Heather."

"Oh, I know what I'm talking about," she said. "I know that when Jesus gave the Great Commission, he didn't say anything about going and making disciples *if* you have a supernatural gift and can hear what he can hear. He didn't say anything about that, Jake, and the Bible doesn't say anything about having special powers to hear people's souls. That was something he threw out to you, for some reason, and I happen to believe it was for a good reason, and a good purpose, and that God knew what he was doing. He didn't make a mistake choosing you, Jake. Not unless you waste the rest of your life away going back to what you were before." And with that, she stormed out of the living room and went to help her mother in the kitchen.

Too angry to eat, Jake burst through the kitchen himself, said, "Mom, I'm going out for a little while," and before she could answer he was in his car pulling out of the driveway.

He drove around for a while, praying and crying, and mumbling under his breath answers to the things Heather had said, as if she were there. He relived the conversation over and over, thinking of clever comebacks.

After a while, he got hungry and decided to go into a McDonald's, harboring the vaguest hope that maybe he had jumped to conclusions. Maybe the gift just had a glitch and wasn't working yesterday. Maybe today it was back. He went in and stood among the people, listening. But he couldn't hear anything. He'd been right—everything had changed.

He could hear the children asking for Happy Meals and ice cream. He could hear the hum of the air conditioner. He could hear people whispering and joking with each other, and the sound of French fries sizzling in grease. He could hear the fizz of the sodas being poured and the rattle of paper as the tables were being bussed. But it was all surface noise. Like ripples on the top of the water. But there was so much underneath, so much he couldn't hear, so many needs that God could hear. So many people weeping and crying out for help, and he couldn't help them.

As he stood in line, waiting to get his order, he whispered under his breath, "I want to hear, Lord. Please let me hear."

But there was nothing. Only the hopeless, sick feeling that he would never get that glimpse again and that, for the rest of his life, all he would hear was empty, useless chatter.

twenty-one

Because Heather's words had haunted him all afternoon, Jake decided to show up at the evangelism class at church. He could sit at the back of the room, he thought, and just be there for moral support. That way Gary would stop riding him about it.

But when he walked in and saw L. J., the black guy who worked behind the counter at the arcade, he started getting excited. Did this hardened gang member really want to share Christ? Andy approached him at the door. "Man, where were you this morning? You wouldn't believe all the people that came. That guy L. J. was looking for you."

"That's amazing," Jake said. "I thought he was coming to church on a dare. Because I challenged him . . ."

"God did the rest," Andy said. "And he has people he wants to tell."

Logan came up behind him. "Gary said we could cut the class short and take some vans to the mall. We thought we could spread out and talk to people."

Jake started feeling sick. He didn't want to spray down their enthusiasm, but witnessing without his gift terrified him. His hands began to sweat, and he slid them into his pockets. How long would it take before they found out he was a fraud? That he was helpless to do anything for God at all.

He stepped inside and saw Lee Grange sitting on the end of the row. The quarterback grinned and shook his hand. "Hey, man. Betcha never thought you'd see me in a class like this."

Jake only grinned. "Good to see you here, Grange."

"I've been reading the Bible, and you know what? We win. Every knee shall bow, every tongue confess. I like being on a winning team."

Jake didn't feel much like a winner.

Gary went to the front of the room and tapped the mike that was more for the sake of getting their attention than for making him easier to hear. "Okay, you guys," he said, quieting them all down. He laughed. "Man, it's so good to see you all here. I can't tell you what an answered prayer it is. You know, I wasn't going to tell you this, but—" he met Jake's eyes, then looked back over the group. "Couple of weeks ago, I was just about ready to turn in my resignation."

A collective gasp came from the students, and he nodded. "It's true. I thought I wasn't making an impact, despite all my prayers. I prayed hard about it, and now look at this." He blinked back the tears in his eyes. "I'm just overwhelmed, guys." He fought back his emotion, then started up again. "Okay, so we're not going to spend a lot of time going over classroom work today. Instead, we're gonna pile into the vans and go to the mall. Anybody have any questions?"

Grange raised his hand.

"Yeah, man."

Grange shifted in his seat. "Well . . . like, how do you do it? Don't you have a playbook or something?"

Everyone laughed. "Great question, Grange," he said. "There's no playbook, but . . ." He seemed to think that over for a while as his eyes scanned the group, and finally, his gaze rested on Jake. "Tell you what, let's get Jake up here. He's the one who's been bringing so many people. He even talked to some of you in here. Jake, come up here and tell us your secret."

Jake's mouth fell open. He couldn't believe his youth pastor would put him on the spot this way, and he certainly hadn't expected him to blurt out that he had a secret, much less that he should give it away. He felt his face reddening, and he shook his head.

Gary coaxed him. "Come on, man. Just come on up."

Jake felt like an idiot, sitting there, stubbornly refusing to go. Finally, he got up and shuffled to the front. The crowd broke out in applause, and he stood there, looking at the floor as they clapped for him, as if he had run the winning touchdown or something. He glanced up and saw Heather. She was the only one not clapping, and she was staring at him with daring eyes, waiting.

You make me sick, she had said today. And he understood it, because he made himself sick.

As they kept clapping, Heather got up from her place on the front row and leaned close to his ear. "Jake, they'll listen to you," she said. "You know what to do, because you taught me. Just tell them." She sat back down.

Gary tapped his shoulder as the applause continued. Jake turned, his eyes shooting daggers. Gary was still grinning. "Man," he said, leaning in against Jake's ear. "I didn't mean you had to tell them that secret. But you learned some things, Jake. Just think about it for a minute and tell us what you can."

The applause died down and the room got quiet, and Jake cleared his throat. "Well . . . uh . . . you see . . ." He cleared it again. "I guess it all just kind of boils down to one thing . . . listening. See, everybody has a spiritual need, and some of them are awful. People out there who feel alone." He glanced at Grange. "People who feel like losers." He scanned the crowd, and his eyes rested on L. J. "Some of them feel like they're being swallowed up by the darkness. Some of them feel like they're dying one second at a time." His eyes met Trina's. She was practically glowing as she smiled up at him. "Some of them have abuse in their past. Some are just alone. But . . . whatever the need is . . . sometimes you can find out those needs by just talking to them. Sometimes you can just look in their face and see the emptiness. Sometimes you can just assume it." He was nervous, and he reached up and scratched his head and dusted a piece of lint off of his pants. He looked back at Gary, wishing he would tell him to go sit back down.

But Gary was still waiting, listening, as if he had something to learn, as well. He looked out over the group again and saw that a girl was raising her hand. "What if we can't figure out their spiritual need?" she asked. "What if they're, like, happy and having fun?"

He had wondered that himself. "You can't go by that," he said. "A person can be standing there cheering at a football game and boozing it up, and you never know that inside their heart's crying out that they have no place to go and no one to turn to." He coughed, just trying to buy more time to think. "They all have the needs, everyone of them. You just have to try to listen with the Holy Spirit's ears."

"How do you know what to say once you get there?" someone else asked.

"The first time I did it," he said, "I opened my mouth and didn't know what was going to come out, and God just gave me the words. Tell them what Jesus did for you. That's the answer. The only one, really, to all their questions. All their needs. They all come down to that one thing." As he said the words, a realization struck him with the force of an electrical shock. He took a step back and pulled his hands out of his pockets.

Could it be? he thought. Could it be that everyone had the same need? Despite the suicidal tendencies, the hate, the loneliness, the sad memories, the hunger . . . Could *all* of those be offshoots of the very same need?

He glanced at Gary as his own eyes came alive. "You know, come to think of it, as many different needs as the people out there have, I think . . . maybe . . . that it all comes down to only one. Every lost soul has the same basic need—they all need Jesus Christ."

It was the first time he had said the words, the first time he had even grasped them. Now that they were out, he had to stand back and think about them for a moment, let the words sink into his subconscious that had been so bent on his being a fraud, so afraid to approach anyone again. But this new information changed a lot of things.

"See, if we all have the Holy Spirit in us, then we're already sensitive to those people. If we can walk up to them, assuming that what they really need, deep down in the deepest part of their soul, is Jesus Christ, then we know what to say. That's a no-brainer."

The crowd sat quietly as each one digested that critical information. Jake let it digest too and felt the reality of it, the truth of it, seep through his veins and fill him with the courage he thought had departed with the gift.

Another hand went up, and Jake nodded. "What if they're Christians already?"

Jake grinned and looked around the room at Andy, Logan, and Heather. "Christians have spiritual needs too," he said. "But now that you mention it, I think those boil down to one too. The Holy Spirit in every Christian wants them to be more like Christ. And for all the lazy, sleeping Christians out there, the ones who aren't bearing any fruit, the ones like me and some of you . . ."

The crowd chuckled.

"What they really want, even though they'll tell you they don't, is to continue the work that Jesus started. That's their purpose. That's what they really want." He glanced over at Gary and saw that his eyes were luminous. Jake knew then that Gary had made his point. Jake *had* learned something in the days that he had the gift. He had learned something he could pass on to others. And he had learned something that would stay with him the rest of his life.

Gary stepped back up to the microphone. "Let's have a word of prayer before we go load the vans."

And as Jake bowed his head, he thanked God that He was still with him.

twenty-two

Jake stood back and let the others climb into the vans first, and it soon became obvious that there wasn't room for him. So, while everyone was trying to cram in, he headed back to his car.

"Hey, Jake!" It was Gary, and Jake looked back over his shoulder and slowed down. "Wait up." Gary ran up to him. "You're not leaving, are you? We need you there."

"No, I'm not leaving. I'll follow behind you guys."

"You did great in there," Gary said. "It was exactly the kind of thing I hoped you'd say. Just what I'd been praying you'd learn."

Jake looked into his eyes. "I didn't know that when I got up to speak. About the bottom line being Jesus and all."

"I know you didn't," Gary said. "But you don't have to worry about what you know and don't know. Like you said, God will do it. I'll see you at the mall."

Jake got into his car and waited until the vans pulled out, and as he drove, he tried to run everything back through his mind. He couldn't get past the fear, despite all the miracles that had happened in his life, all the ways God had worked through him and in him. The fear was paralyzing him. He was afraid to walk up to some stranger and start a conversation when he didn't know what was going on in their hearts. He felt like Andy and Logan must have felt a few days ago, when he'd been sitting there hammering home their need to bear fruit and they had found every excuse in the book not to.

"I don't want to make excuses," he whispered, knowing God heard every word. "I want to be as bold as I was, but I'm different now." He hit his hand on the steering wheel and looked up into the cloudy sky. "Lord, show me how to hear without the voices. Show me how to look into their souls and see what you see."

He waited until everyone had piled out of the vans, and he sat there a moment, thinking they were all expecting him to be leader of the pack, when he was shaking harder than any of them. He got out and followed them as they headed up to the doors. Heather fell back.

"You okay?" she whispered.

He shrugged. "Just nervous."

She touched his arm. "Hey, I'm sorry for all the things I said to you. I mean, they were true, and I'm glad I said them. I'm just sorry they were true so I *had* to say them."

"You're not making any sense."

"You did good in there," she said. "The things you said . . . If you don't think God's still with you, you aren't thinking."

"Thanks," he said.

"And you know, if Andy can do this, you can."

He looked up ahead and saw his buddies leading the charge. They couldn't wait to get in there and start reliving the victories they had lived the night before.

Some stopped in at the arcade, and others walked down the mall, looking for people who needed to know about Jesus.

Jake followed the dozen or so into the arcade and hung back at the door, watching as his friends, some old, some new, spread out and started conversations with various kids at the machines. Jake thought of running out, of going back to his car and going home. No one would ever know. They would think he was just out somewhere where they couldn't see, leading dozens of people to Christ. He could probably get away with that for a little while.

Then he felt guilty, because he knew that his main motivation was not to look stupid in front of his friends. But hadn't he learned days ago that embarrassment was a small price to pay when Jesus had hung on a cross for him? For all of these people in here? What was it Trina had said Friday night?

But who cares what they say? A man died. And he rose again. So really, what difference does it make if people laugh at us. We've got him on our side, and one day, they're gonna find out for sure, one way or another.

He saw a kid standing off to the side with his hands in his pockets, his dull eyes scanning the games and machines.

Slowly, Jake started to approach him. He didn't say anything right away, just went to stand next to him and looked out over the people. "You waiting for a machine?" he asked finally.

The boy shrugged. "I don't have any money."

Jake nodded. "I like to come in and just watch too sometimes."

The boy glanced up at him. "Really, I just came to get away from my dad and his girlfriend. They're shopping for jewelry."

Jake grinned. "You don't like his girlfriend, or do you just have something against jewelry?"

"Both," the kid said. "I can take her or leave her. I'm only here for a couple of days."

But Jake knew exactly what the boy was going through. He had those visits with his father once a year, when he and Heather got on a plane and headed across the country to spend three or four days there. His father didn't even bother to take the time off work.

He reached his hand into a pocket and pulled out some change. "I was about to buy a Coke. Want one?"

The kid's eyebrows shot up, as if the offer surprised him. "Yeah, thanks."

He pushed off from the wall and headed for the concession stand and bought the two drinks. He turned to see the kid standing beside him, then handed him his drink and leaned back against the wall. "You know, my parents can be a real downer sometimes too," Jake said. "They've been divorced about five years, and my dad's remarried. Whenever I visit him, I feel more like an unwanted guest than his son."

"I know just how you feel," the kid said, as if he was the one trying to make Jake feel better.

"My mom's okay, though," Jake said. "She does the best she can."

"Mine too," the kid acknowledged.

Jake sipped on his drink. "But I finally figured out that my life doesn't have to hang on theirs. You know how people are; they always let you down."

He could see in the kid's face that he was relating to what Jake was saying. He kept drinking, but his gaze drifted down to the floor.

"But I found somebody else who won't ever let me down."

The kid's eyes met Jake's, and Jake knew he had gotten his attention. Jake had the answer, the cure, but he suddenly felt panicked. What if he couldn't do this? What if he said the wrong thing and drove him away? What if the kid thought he had only befriended him so he could give him a sales pitch?

He looked around, almost searching for help. Andy was standing close by, but he was in a deep conversation with Byrd the Nerd from their school, in front of a video game. He was sure it was the first time Andy had talked to the guy. He looked across the room and saw L. J. talking to a bulked-up jock in a letterman's jacket. They, too, were in deep conversation, and the jock was hanging on to every word. Unbelievable, Jake thought. A former gang member talking to a jock about grace. Only changed people could do something this bold.

Then he saw movement at the corner of his eye, and Zeke, the Goth who'd fought with Grange, strode into the room. Jake heard a flurry of whispers and saw Grange turn around. Jake straightened and touched the kid's shoulder, as if to protect him if this went bad. But Zeke's eyes met Grange's, and he stiffened like a cowboy staring down his enemy, as if deciding which one would leave town before sundown.

And then Grange held out his hand to shake.

Zeke didn't take it right away. He just looked at it, his eyes hard, piercing.

Then Grange started talking, and even though he couldn't hear, Jake knew he was apologizing for what had happened the other night.

"Who is it?" the kid asked him.

Jake glanced back at the kid he'd been talking to. "What?"

"Who is that person you were telling me about, who won't let me down?"

Jake remembered what he was doing. He glanced back up at Grange and Zeke and saw that Zeke's hardness seemed to be melting away, and now all he saw was a sad vulnerability and a hunger as he looked into Grange's face.

Would Grange lead Zeke to Christ? Could there be a miracle that huge?

Jake didn't know, but suddenly, he had the confidence that he needed. God was with him, just as he was with the gangster who witnessed to the hulk, and the brain who was witnessing to a nerd. He was with the jock who was witnessing to a Goth.

He saw his sister talking to the mother of a kid who was playing pinball. Heather smiled at him, urging him to go on.

Yes, if God was with them, he was with Jake.

And as he turned back and looked into the boy's face, Jake realized he had everything it took to lead this kid to Christ. He wore his needs right there on the surface. In his face, in his stance, in the way he carried himself. In his very words.

And what Jake couldn't hear, the Holy Spirit could. He could do what Jake could not.

This boy needed Christ. And that was all Jake needed to know.

YOUTH LEADERS!

If you'd like to challenge your youth group
to be heart readers, go to **www.theheartreader.com**
or **www.wpublishinggroup.com**.

There you'll find exercises designed to help students
• see the real needs of the people around them
• learn the bare bones basics of sharing their faith and
• understand the natural obstacles to witnessing.

All this told through an easy-to-understand
story students can relate to.